THE *CALEB* CHRONICLES

Pastor D. W. Riffe

Copyright © 2023 **Pastor D. W. Riffe Publishing**

All rights reserved. No part of this publication may be reproduced, distributed, or transmitted in any form or by any means, including photocopying, recording, or other electronic or mechanical methods, without the prior written permission of the publisher, except in the case of brief quotations embodied in critical reviews and certain other noncommercial uses permitted by copyright law. For permission requests, write to the publisher, addressed "Attention: Book Rights and Permission," at the address below.

Published in the United States of America

ISBN 978-1-962110-43-3 (SC)
ISBN 978-1-962730-99-0 (HC)

Pastor D. W. Riffe Publishing
222 West 6th Street
Suite 400, San Pedro, CA, 90731
pastordwriffe@outlook.com

Ordering Information and Rights Permission:

Quantity sales. Special discounts might be available on quantity purchases by corporations, associations, and others. For details, contact the publisher at the address above.

For Book Rights Adaptation and other Rights Permission. Call us at toll-free 1-888-945-8513 or send us an email at admin@stellarliterary.com.

DEDICATION

This book is dedicated to my wife who went to be with her Lord on 02/21/2023. The character of Wah'li'si is based on her. She encouraged me to purser this dream.

This book is also dedicated to my son Caleb Elijah Joe Riffe, who went to be with the Timeless-One on January 26, 1995. He was only two and a half months old but turned my world upside down. He was attacked by a rare muscular disease called myo-tubular myopathy. I can't wait to see him again.

Also, I would like to dedicate this book to my mom and dad who went on to be with their Lord. He was a great, and a very wise man. And she was the godliest woman I ever knew. They lived their faith, and I thank God they did. I would hate to think where I would have ended up without God in our home.

CONTENTS

DEDICATION iii
ACKNOWLEDGMENTS v
INTRO: vi
1 THE INVITATION 1
2 THE BLACK DOME 13
3 THE STORY 23
4 THE FIRE 30
5 THECONTEST 40
6 THE SOUND OF SILENCE 57
7 RHYME, RIDDLES AND REASON 74
8 THE GARDEN 82
9 DREAMS 101
10 LIQUID CHRIST 108
11 THE VISION OF A SATANIC INTERVIEW 120
12 CORRIDORS 127
13 THE PSALMUS 139
14 PORTAL 145
15 AS THE DANCERS DANCE 169
16 BEFORE ANCIENT PSALMUS 2 184
SONGS AND PRAYERS OF A WARRIOR PRIEST 198
WHAT IS OUTCAST NATION? 226
ABOUT THE AUTHOR 230

ACKNOWLEDGMENTS

I would like to thank all those who helped me in getting this project off the ground. First my wife Claudine for sticking with me and encouraging me to keep going and not give up. To my daughters Stephanie and Emily for the input about how a computer works. To my mother for all the encouraging words. And to my editors, Melissa Rossborough and Sheila Riffe, thank you very much.

INTRO:

Once upon a time…No, wait; in a time yet to come… Or maybe; in a time, unknown to the world, lived a man in a small community called High Rock. The man: Caleb -- High Priest, Warrior and Worship Leader for the people of High Rock.

Caleb, a quiet man, does not speak idle words and only speaks when necessary. He stands about six feet tall and has shoulder blade length black hair. He is thirty-two years old and unmarried at the time of this writing. He is very spiritual and worships only the Lord of all; the Creator of the Universe and beyond; the One who was never born and will never die -- The Timeless-One. Caleb doesn't just pray to the Timeless-One; he does what is known as heart-linking. This is a very intimate and powerful way to talk with the Timeless-One and to bring your needs to Him. Caleb heart-links no less than three times a day. He is also the chief spiritual leader of High Rock. The people love Caleb dearly, and the children adore him and love to hear him tell stories.

High Rock is a community of about three thousand people. It lies in the middle of Mount Triune. Mount Triune cannot be found on any map, for the Timeless-One has hidden it from the world. There exists a visible protective force around High Rock. In the day it looks as though it is raining crystal and silver flakes on the mountain. At night it looks as though it is on fire. The people call this "the protective hand of the Timeless-One".

No evil can enter High-Rock, unless allowed by the Timeless-One, and then the evil has no power. There is only one way to get to High Rock. One must climb the east side of Mount Triune to about halfway up, until he comes to a road that leads around the backside of the mountain. There, one comes to a cave opening. This is the beginning of a path that leads straight through the mountain and comes out at the edge of the village of High Rock where there is a gate made of different precious metals. The gate itself can only be opened by the power of the Spirit of the Timeless-One. High Rock lies right in the middle of Mount Triune. Mount Triune is three mountains in one and surrounds the valley on the mountain that flows with milk, honey and complete peace. The Timeless-One reigns in High Rock.

The people there are peaceful and gentle. They do not need to work, for the Timeless-One provides their every need. This is paradise outside of Heaven. And this mountain valley village called High Rock is where the High Priest, Caleb begins his adventures. Here is where Caleb and holy regime who are Wah'li'si, Christopher, Logan, Eli'Zur, Saleah and Zoe begin their missions to other dimensions, to the underworld, to unknown regions of the world to battle evil and to bring the lost to the Timeless-One.

Here are just a few of Caleb's adventures; we call them the Caleb Chronicles.

1
THE INVITATION

"Blessed is the man

Who walks not in the counsel of the ungodly

Nor stands in the path of sinners

Nor sits in the seat of the scornful

But his delight is in the Law of the Lord

And in his Law he meditates day and night"

Psalm 1:1, 2 NKJV

As he lifted his hands and eyes to the Timeless-One, he opened his mouth. Although there were no words, a smoke like vapor rose from him. This is the incense of the heart-link to the Timeless-One. The heart-link is a very sacred and important practice for the people of High Rock. A people set apart from the rest of the world for the service and worship of the Timeless-One.

This day as Caleb was in the courtyard in the cool morning, he was in heart-link with the Timeless-One when a small girl and boy ran up to him out of breath with a message in his hand. It was from the magician who lives in the Valley of the Seven Death Fountains. The girl and boy had been playing by the gate of Precious Metals when a creature in the form of a little girl appeared on the other side. The creature said while sliding the letter through the bars of the gate, "Boy?! Little girl, would you please give this very important letter to Caleb the High Priest?" The boy walked over and said while reaching out to take the letter, "How did you get out there?" As soon as he took the letter the little girl vanished. The girl and boy gave the letter to Caleb. The message was written on a material unknown to the people of High Rock. "Where did you get this Lily? Ben, where did you get this?" Breathless Ben answered saying, "A girl gave it to me from the other side of the gate. Caleb, I don't think she..." Caleb interrupted Ben and said, "I know. Thank you, now run along home and get some lunch." Caleb messed Ben's hair up and patted him on the back and he and Lily ran off.

Caleb turned the letter over several times to examine it, and then opened it. It read as follows.

"To Caleb, High Priest of the people of High Rock and servant to the Timeless-One,
Greetings,
I would like to invite you to my humble dwelling place to discuss a matter of great importance to you and your people. I look forward to meeting with you.
Sincerely,
Mr. Wizard."

Caleb reread the letter several times, and then went back to heart-linking with the Timeless-One.

At first, Caleb did not want to go see Mr. Wizard, nor did he want to talk with him. He did not want to be near where he lived at all. But, out of concern for the people of High Rock he decided to go and hear what Mr. Wizard had to say. Caleb lifted his hands and his eyes toward heaven and said, "Oh Timeless-One, Your will be done. My heart says go. What does Your heart say?" The Timeless-One answered Caleb saying, "Caleb, my friend, go to Mr. Wizard for he loves darkness and hates the Light. He clings to evil and curses Love. Before he causes one of my little ones to fall, you must go." Caleb fell to his knees in worship.

The journey to the Valley of the Seven Death Fountains was a day's travel by foot. It was another half a day's travels to Mr. Wizard's dwelling place. Two days later as he started to leave, he saw Saleah and Zoe in the courtyard entertaining the little girls with dance and singing. Saleah and Zoe are cousins, they are both in their late teens, "Saleah, Zoe." Caleb called.

"Yes Caleb? Are you going someplace?" asked the girls. "Yes," said Caleb. "I must leave for a few days. Would you tell Wah'li'si I will see her on the Day of Praise." "You're not going out of High Rock, are you?" asked Zoe. "It will be fine, the Timeless-One has gone on before me." said Caleb. "We will tell Wah'li'si." said Saleah. A few hours into his journey, he began singing a song,

"Oh Timeless-One
I know you are with me,
I know you are beside me,
I know you dwell in me.

Oh Timeless-One,
I heart-link with you,

I worship only you,
I will die for you."

Caleb had decided before he set out on his journey that he would not eat or drink anything until after his meeting with Mr. Wizard. He wanted to keep himself focused and clean, pure in thought and deed, solely relying on the Timeless-One for guidance in word and action. About halfway to the valley, Caleb saw a man sitting within a circle on the ground about a stone's throw away. There was a blue glow surrounding the man and the circle. This was a protective force for the man against the evil he invokes. In front of the man was a lit black candle. It was lit, but it gave no light. The man said nothing as he looked up with eyes full of blackness at Caleb and grinned an evil grin. Just then from behind Caleb came a loud and awful noise. As Caleb turned around, he saw smoke and fire coming out of the ground. Then from out of the ground with a shriek came three black hideous looking creatures. They stood about six feet tall and looked like shadows. Their eyes were sockets filled with a green glow. Their faces were skulls with patches of flesh hanging off them.

They had long black hair and wore long red robes with wide black belts. Their hands looked like the claws of dragons. There was also a strong stench of death coming from them.

Then one of the creatures spoke to Caleb in a voice that seemed forward and sounded backward at the same time saying, "My name is Mephistopheles. This is Lucifuge and this is Asmodeus.

We **are** the crown princes of **hell!** We have been summoned to kill you! For you serve the Timeless-One." Caleb answered saying, "You cannot touch me. You do not have the power or the authority to do such a thing." The man is still sat in his protecting circle, legs crossed in a lotus position staring into the candle. As the three creatures began circling Caleb, they were hissing and chanting, using a language unknown to Caleb. Caleb lifted his hands, palms up, head tilted back. Then he said, "Oh, Timeless-One. Rescue me. Show your awesome power and glory." At that instant, an intensely bright white light came down on Caleb from heaven like a laser. The light made a pulsing, humming sound. The creatures covered their eyes and cried out in pain. Caleb stood still, with hands lifted, palms up, head tilted back and looking up to heaven.

Mephistopheles yelled at the man in the circle saying, "Send us back! Send us back from where we came!" From out of the light and out of the humming came a voice saying, "Caleb, my friend, you are always in my grip." Then suddenly, beams like lasers shot out from the light that surrounded Caleb slicing through the creatures like a two-edged sword cutting through a wax candle. Once the pieces of the creatures hit the ground they were no more. They vanished. Then the light shot back up into the heavens. Caleb looked over where the man sat in the protective circle. The man was gone. All that was left was a pile of ash where the man sat. Caleb stood there and heart-linked with the Timeless-One.

Caleb then pressed on. As night set in he came to the edge of the Valley of the Seven Death Fountains. There he saw another creature sitting on a large bolder. The creature sat with his legs crossed.

He had giant bat like wings that were stretched out. He had the head of goat with an inverted pentagram on his forehead. Between his horns, coming out of his head was a flame of fire like that of a torch. He spoke to Caleb saying, "My name is Baphomet, I am the end of your journey. This is where you will breathe your last breath." Caleb replied saying, "I do not know you. Why do you wish me harm?"

"Because you worship the Timeless-One of course." answered Baphomet.

"I am to meet with Mr. Wizard, Baphomet. Let me be, and I will be on my way." said Caleb. Raising his left hand, Baphomet said, "Don't think I am some naïve magician sitting in a protective circle, casting black spells and invoking demons to do my bidding. I am a god. Witches, warlocks and magicians worship me. I am full of all the power that exists in the darkened spirit plane. My power is great, and my words bring death!"

Caleb then responded by saying in a calm but authoritative voice, "A god you may be, but God you are not. I serve the Timeless-One and only He do I serve. He has called me to be a high priest and a warrior. He has touched my heart, my mind and my soul. He that is touched by the Timeless-One cannot be touched by evil. You, Baphomet, are pure evil and have no business being on this planet. But then again maybe you do have a reason -- to show everyone that the Timeless-One is all powerful and you are nothing more than a fly that needs to be squashed."

Baphomet laughed an evil laugh and said," You speak empty words high priest. I am Baphomet god of the witches, ruler of the black air and prince of pain! You will die!" Baphomet took his left hand and drew an inverted pentagram in the air while speaking a chant backwards saying," Eid lliw uoy belac, rewop ym yb!" Caleb at the same time was heart-linking with the Timeless-One.

Baphomet began chanting louder and tracing the inverted pentagram faster and faster.

A blue light began circling Baphomet with the sound of a roaring wind mixed with the sounds of backward demonic voices saying," belac eid, belac eid!!" The words had no effect on Caleb, as they got louder and faster. Then the bright white light of the Timeless-One came down on Caleb. Baphomet said," Your God has no power here!" Caleb whipped his head around at Baphomet. Caleb's eyes looked as though they were on fire.

Caleb pointed at him and said, "That's enough! In the name of the Timeless-One, who lives and never dies; who changes the heart of man, but never changes; who is the only God; who is life and brings life to all men.

But to you brings death! Be gone!" Just then, a beam of light shot out from Caleb and went straight through the chest of Baphomet.

Baphomet had just enough time to look down at the hole in his chest just before he exploded into a fine dust. Caleb stood there and sang a song of praise to the Timeless-One.

"Before darkness covered the endless space,
Before your angels sang songs of praise,
You are.
Before you created air,
Before you called for sound,
Before you hung one star,
Before you made one heart to pound,
You are.
Glory to the Timeless-One"

As Caleb stepped into the Valley of the Seven Death Fountains for a moment, he felt sick to his stomach and his spirit was deeply grieved. He stopped where he was and heart-linked with the Timeless- One.

The Timeless-One breathed on him and at once Caleb was at peace and was empowered, energized, and refreshed with the Holy Spirit of the Timeless-One. Caleb sang once again, a song of praise to the Timeless-One.

"Oh how great is your love for your servant,
You breathed on me and gave me power,
You touched my mind and gave me peace,
You broke my heart and made me whole,
Life, love and joy you have given me,

With the fire of your Spirit, You restored my soul,

Holy, holy, holy, to the Timeless-One."

Caleb moved forward and deeper into the valley. He walked on and did not stop until he came to the gate of the dwelling place of Mr. Wizard.

As Caleb walked through the gate, he could see Mr. Wizard's house. It was dark. Everything seemed to be made of shadows. Everywhere Caleb looked he could see bodiless, glowing green eyes watching him. He could hear hissing and whispering but could not understand them. Just before he reached the door of the house, it opened on its own. Just on the other side standing in a darkened room, facing the door, dressed in black from head to toe was Mr. Wizard. He stood about six feet tall, long black hair (about mid-way down his back), also a goatee. His build was very thin, with ghostly pale skin and eyes as black as coal. Mr. Wizard walked to the door and said," Welcome Caleb, high priest and servant to the Timeless-One. Please come in. I'm so glad you came."

Caleb walked through the door and said, "Thank you."

Looking around the darkened room illuminated only by a few candles Caleb could see and feel the evil around him. On one wall Caleb saw an inverted pentagram with a black candle on either side of it. On another wall, he saw an upside-down cross and hanging next to it was the Lord's Prayer written backwards. At this point Caleb became very angry.

As he continued looking, he saw a doorway to another room. As he walked over to it he saw on the floor a huge circle with a pentagram inside. Each point touched the circle and at each point was a lit candle. In the center was an altar. Hanging above the altar was an inverted cross.

Caleb turned and faced Mr. Wizard and said demandingly, "Speak! Why did you want me here?" Just then, a black cat raced over and sprang into Mr. Wizard's arms. Mr. Wizard began stroking the cat and sneered, "I just wanted to know one thing. What are you going to do to stop me?"

"Stop you from what?" Caleb replied.

Mr. Wizard bent down and gently put the cat on the floor. As he slowly stood back-up he softly said, "Conjuring. Spell casting. Bloody sacrifice. Killing."

"What are you talking about?" Caleb said sternly.

"What am I talking about?" Mr. Wizard replied. " I am going to destroy High Rock and all who inhabit it, with a single curse."

"Do you really think you have the power to do that?" asked Caleb.

"Oh, I do, I do" replied Mr. Wizard arrogantly. "And I'll tell you why" Mr. Wizard started pacing as he spoke, "As I was in meditation, the Dark One came to me in a vision in the form of a dragon on the astral plane. He told me that if I am to become the most powerful wizard that ever lived, I had to perform one last task." Walking over to a table nearby he picked up his magic wand and continued speaking, "I am to cast a simple spell on the good people of High Rock. Of course, that spell will bring death. Before you say anything, I need to tell you, that I must first kill their High Priest. This is why you are here Caleb. Ha, ha, ha." Mr. Wizard laughed.

"You have no power over me or the people of High Rock!" Caleb replies. "You are not worth my time. I will be leaving now."

As Caleb started walking toward the door, Mr. Wizard lifted his left hand and from across the room the door slammed shut. Caleb whipped his head around toward Mr. Wizard and with complete authority in his voice said, "You don't want to do this!" Just then, the room began to glow with a light. Caleb raised his hands, palms up, and tilted his head back and began heart-linking with the Timeless-One.

Mr. Wizard laughed and said, "Your God, the Timeless-One, has no power here! Your incense cannot penetrate the force of protection! You will die here! Then the world will know that Mr. Wizard has been granted, all power and has been given full and absolute power from the Old One, the Dragon.... Leviathan!"

Caleb remained in heart-link with the Timeless-One as Mr. Wizard began to walk around him chanting, "Cursed is the Timeless-One! Cursed is Caleb! Die you will, die you must! Blessed be the Dragon! So mote it be!"

With his head tilted back and mouth opened, a smoke-like mist came out of Caleb's mouth with no words or sound. This is the incense of his prayer. While Mr. Wizard continued chanting and circling Caleb, an intensely bright white light came down on Caleb penetrating the blue force like a bolt of lightning. It covered him like a cloud. Mr. Wizard fell back from the force of the light.

Caleb dropped his hands and swung around to look at Mr. Wizard. Caleb's eyes burned red with the power of the Holy Fire. Caleb took two steps toward Mr. Wizard as he lay on the floor and said, "The Timeless-One, the one who speaks with the voice of Seven Thunders says to you Mr. Wizard, 'I will no longer wait to smell the aroma of your incense. This day, this hour you shall be with your master Dragon in his fiery den of everlasting pain and suffering. Prepare for your journey to the sea of death, for it will be swift."

Mr. Wizard stood to his feet and began chanting again. With much fear, he cast a circle of protection around himself and called out to Dragon, "Great Dragon I call on you to slay this enemy of ours! Send me Legion so we may conquer this priest and his people and his God!"

Caleb stepped closer to Mr. Wizard and spoke again saying, "Mr. Wizard your circle will not protect you. Your words fall to the ground just as you are about to do. Your master has abandoned you like a coward."

Caleb now circled around Mr. Wizard and said, "You have chosen your path, now follow it! Take your journey home. The other side of life awaits your arrival. Now go!"

Just then Mr. Wizard fell to the floor. Then there was a shaking of the ground as the floor broke apart to reveal a large hole in the ground. Heat and smoke rose out of it. Just then demons reached up from the pit and grabbed Mr. Wizard pulling and ripping at his flesh, dragging him into its mouth screaming. Then he was no more.

Caleb walked out of the house and saw the sun rising. The trees now had green leaves and the air was sweet. The shadow eyes were gone, and the evil was no longer in that place. Caleb stood there for a moment and sang a song of praise to the Timeless-One.

"You never forget your servant,
You never forsake your child,
You are with me in the calm times,
You are with me in the trial.
Blessed is the Timeless-One,
Blessed is your name,
Blessed is the Timeless-One,
Holy is your name,
You delivered me from evil,
You delivered me from pain,
You sheltered me from death,
You are the only way."

Caleb journeyed back to High Rock safely. When he arrived, the people gathered in the yard to hear of his great adventure and of his deliverance from all the attacks of evil. Ben and Lily ran to Caleb and hugged him and said," We were praying for you Caleb."

"I know you were guys; I know you were." replied Caleb. Zoe, Saleah and Wah'li'si walked up to Caleb and said, "Just in time for the Day of Praise." "Cutting it close uh, Caleb?" said Wah'li'si.

The people worshipped together and gave thanks to the Timeless-One for the safe return of their High Priest and for the Lord's awesome power.

To be continued…

2

THE BLACK DOME

"Brethren if anyone among you,
wanders from the truth, and someone,
turns him back let him know that he who turns
a sinner from the error of his way
will save a soul from death and
cover a multitude of sin."

James 5:19, 20

"Caleb? Hello? Are you here?" asked Eli'Zur as he entered the Temple. He is Bishop under Caleb, the High Priest of High Rock. He is forty-two years old; about five foot ten, bald and very muscular.

Caleb came from around the corner out of his office and said with a smile, "Eli'Zur! Welcome, how was your trip?"

"It was good, but there…." replied Eli'Zur as Caleb interrupts, "How many were rescued?"

"Thirty-seven" replied Eli'Zur.

"That's great. Very good, and where is my brother? Did he go on home?" asked Caleb.

"Caleb there is something I need to tell you." said Eli'Zur.

Caleb walked toward Eli'Zur and put his hands on Eli' Zur's shoulders and said, "Tell me. What is wrong?"

Eli'Zur stepped back, turned around, and said, "It's your brother."

"What about Logan? What has happened? Where is he?" asked Caleb.

Eli'Zur explained, "After the rescue, Logan, Seth and Nathan left camp to spy on the Dark Eyes. They didn't take their Spirit Swords with them. They must have gotten careless. They were captured by the Dark Eyes."

"What are you saying Eli'Zur?!" Caleb demanded.

"They were taken prisoner. They're in the Black Dome without their Spirit Swords. I'm sorry Caleb." Eli'Zur said with sorrow.

Caleb put his hands over his face and took a deep breath. He looked up at Eli'Zur with a fire in his eyes and a firm voice and said, "We will get them out!" Caleb walked toward Eli'Zur and said, "Go home and get some rest."

As Eli'Zur walked away he stopped, turned around and said, "I'm sorry Caleb. I should have been a better leader. I'm sorry."

"It's not your fault Eli'Zur. Now go home and get some rest. Go on now" Caleb replied.

After Eli'Zur left, Caleb walked over to the altar called Stillness and lifted his hands, palms up, and tilted his head back to heart-link with the Timeless-One. No words are spoken during the heart-link, just spirit and Spirit becoming one with a smoke-like vapor rising from his mouth. After he is finished, he sang a song to the Timeless-One.

"Oh Timeless-One
Creator of all
Full of power
I hear the call.
You have no beginning

You have no end
You are wisdom
On you I depend"

The next day Caleb and Eli'Zur gathered ten of the most devoted followers of the Timeless-One and told them of the mission they were about to embark on.

Caleb said to the men, "As you know three of our men have been taken by the Dark Eyes and taken into the Black Dome. We intend to get them out of there."

Caleb stood to his feet and walked around the men, putting his hands on their shoulders and speaking, "It will be dangerous. You must stay in constant heart-link with the Timeless-One. There must be no distractions and no fear! The enemy is strong, but the Timeless-One will go before us. We will be victorious. Let us heart-link."

When they were finished, they set out on the journey to the Black Dome. The journey took three and a half days travel by foot. They stopped at a safe distance and camped overnight. When morning came, they all got up just before sun rise. They built a fire and Caleb read from the Holy Verses. Then they all joined in a Sacred Song for deliverance:

"Oh, Timeless-One
Oh, Holy One
Carry us through
And guide our Swords
Oh, Timeless-One
Power and Spirit
Lift us up

Bring the enemy to their knees"

Afterward Caleb said, "Let us heart-link to the Timeless-One and meditate on His mighty power and love." So they all gathered in a circle and heart-linked to the Timeless-One. The aroma of the incense of the heart-link was very pleasing to the Timeless-One. When they had finished Caleb spoke to them again saying, "For those of you who have never seen or been to the Black Dome let me tell you some things about it."

They all sat down as Caleb began telling them about the Black Dome. "It looks like a big black bubble. It is five miles in diameter and is watched by the Dark Eyes. The Dark Eyes watch people and looks into the heart and soul. They can tell who are weak in spirit, and who are double minded. Those are the ones they entice, trap and pull into the Black Dome.

Once inside they can never leave, nor do they want to. The only way out is with the Spirit Sword." Caleb continues, "The people in the Dome have no idea where they are, nor do they feel anything is wrong. And as far as they know nothing exists outside the Dome. Now I want to warn you, you will see and hear things that you have only read about -- pure evil and pure sin. This is life without God. You will see things that the people in the Dome can't see. Fear not for the Timeless-One is with us."

"How do we get inside?" asked Timothy, one of the ten.

Eli'Zur answered saying, "The Dark Eyes cannot see anyone who is completely filled with the Holy Spirit of the Timeless-One and who carries the Spirit Sword in hand. So, we can walk by them with no problem. But, to get inside the Dome is a little tricky. The only way in without being pulled in is to take your Spirit Sword and strike the wall of the Dome. A hole will appear, but only for eight seconds. So, once the hole appears you have eight seconds to jump through the hole before it closes."

Caleb takes over speaking, "Logan, Seth and Nathan will not recognize us so, we are going to have to take them by force."

"Why will they not recognize us?" asked Peter.

"They have been blinded, blinded by the darkness. They are spiritually blinded to the Truth. Darkness has blinded them with their dark light of evil." replied Caleb.

Eli'Zur spoke again, "Be on your guard. Be sober in mind and in heart. The evil inside that dome is powerful and will try to deceive you. They will try to entice you, seduce you and trick you. They will try to kill you. They do this in vain.

The Timeless-One has given us a Spirit of discernment and power. Inside the dome the spirit world becomes physical for us. You will be able to see and hear the tormenting demons. Fear not! The Timeless-One is with us. Use the Spirit Sword. Speak the words of the Timeless-One. Stay strong. All will be well. This rescue will not fail!" The men stood to their feet and clapped and shouted with excitement.

Caleb took his Spirit Sword and lifted it to the Heavens. Eli'Zur and the ten did the same. All twelve Swords touched points in the air. Just then a very bright white light shot down from the Heavens hitting the tips of the Swords. The light went down the Swords like lightening and went into their hands, down their arms and into their bodies.

After three minutes the light shot back up into the Heavens. When the men brought the Spirit Swords down their bodies were glowing with the power of the Timeless-One and their hair had turned pure white. Their hearts were on fire and their bodies were energized with the power of the Timeless-One. Caleb looked at the men with the Fire of the Holy Spirit in his eyes and said with determination in his voice, "Let's do it!" The men shouted a victory shout and headed for the Dome.

When they got to the Dome, they walked right by the Dark Eyes without being seen, just as Eli'Zur had said. One by one they struck the side of the Black Dome and jumped through the opening.

Once inside some of the men got sick to their stomach because of the pure evil that inhabited the Dome. "Focus on the Timeless-One and His love and grace! The evil can't touch you!" said Eli'Zur. At that the men were fine.

They held their Spirit Swords out in front of them for all to see. Then they began their search for the three men. The people in the Dome were like zombies and did not know Caleb and the men were there. The people moved about aimlessly, without direction and without emotion.

The air in the Dome had a stale and lifeless feel to it. It was mid-morning, but inside the Dome it felt like the sun was about to set. It was dark and cold. Although the people couldn't see or hear them, Caleb and the men could see and hear the shadow demons that crawled all over the inhabitants of the Black Dome while picking at their eyes and hearts.

When the shadow demons saw Caleb and the men they started hissing and cursing at them saying, "Ah, Priest, you must leave! You…do not …belong here…Priest! Leave now and we will spare your life…Priest! Stay…and we will…kill you!"

Caleb and the men ignored them and walked on. They stayed together as they searched for Logan, Seth and Nathan.

"Caleb, there are so many" said one of the ten.

"Yes" replied Caleb.

Then a young woman with tears in her eyes walked by them, as though they weren't even there. Crawling on her was a hideous looking demon digging its claws into her flesh and spitting black saliva on her eyes. As soon as the woman got by Caleb and the men, the demon threw a ball of fire at Caleb. Caleb whipped around with his Sword and hit the fire ball turning it into a crystallized powder. Caleb looked at the men and said, "Stay together and stay alert. Our enemy is here and is prowling." Then the men held their Swords up and ready. As they walked on, the shadow demons continued to hiss and curse at them.

The shadow demons varied in shape and size. Some were very hairy, and some were completely bald. Some looked like deformed cats with legs like spiders. Others had the body of a snake with a man's head and teeth of a rat. Still others resembled frogs with scorpion tails. None were over three and a half feet tall. The stench that came from them filled the entire Dome and was almost unbearable. The smell resembled rotting and burning human flesh. The smaller demons crawled and hung on the people and could be seen going in and out of the people's mouths and eyes. And all the while cursing and vomiting at the people and spitting their black saliva.

Caleb, Eli'Zur, along with the ten, pressed on in search of their loved ones continually fighting off fire balls and trying to ignore the blasphemous talk coming from the shadow demons. As they approached a large, dead tree Caleb said, "Let us take a break and rest for a few minutes." When they began to sit down and rest, a woman walked by them with several demons on her. Then suddenly one of the demons jumped off of her onto a branch of the tree that hung in front of Caleb. The demon had the body of a pig, a head of a man and the tail of a monkey.

The demon swung around and hung by its tail in front of Caleb's face and said in a low hissing voice, "Caleb, High Priest to the Timeless-One. What… are you… doing here? Mm hm, mm hm?"

"We are looking for our friends that your Dark Eyes pulled in here." Caleb replied sternly.

"Mm hm, mm hm. Well, they now… belong to us. They… are home… now. Mm hm, mm hm," said the demon.

"Listen little demon…" replied Caleb as the demon interrupted.

"My… name is… Plague."

Caleb continues, "Listen little demon, we are going to find my brother and our friends and leave with them. And we might take a few more people with us!"

"You… may be… High Priest at… High Rock… but… you are… aliens here! And… you… will die… here!" screamed Plague with much anger.

All the while they were talking, shadow demons were circling Caleb and the men. Then Caleb said, "Look Plaque…"

"That's Plague!" interrupted Plague.

Caleb continues speaking saying, "Sorry. Listen Plaque, the Timeless-One is all powerful here and at High Rock, and from the moon and beyond a thousand galaxies." Then Caleb quickly reached out and grabbed Plague by the tail and held him out in front of him. Caleb looked Plague in the eyes and said, "Get out of my way little demon!" and then threw him back into the tree.

Plague grabbed a tree limb by his tail and yelled, "Attack, attack!" The demons spit their black saliva at Caleb and the men and began leaping on them trying to get inside their bodies. Pushing the demons off themselves, they took their Swords and attacked the demons slicing them in half, with one stroke.

The pieces fell to the ground and with a screech joined back together and ran off whimpering. When all the demons were gone Caleb whipped around and sliced Plague in half. Grabbing the piece still hanging on the tree threw it far off away from the other piece that lay on the ground by his feet. Then Caleb turned to Eli'Zur and the ten, "Is everyone o.k.?"

They all answered "Yes."

Caleb then said, "Good. Let us heart-link to the Timeless-One." When they were finished, they were all energized and again pressed on.

It didn't take them long after heart-linking to find their loved ones. When Caleb, Eli'Zur and the ten approached them, Logan and the others didn't recognize them. They were in a daze, and each had a demon on them picking at their flesh. Caleb and the men did not try to talk to them but grabbed the demons that were on them and threw them off. Caleb grabbed Logan, Eli'Zur grabbed Seth and Peter grabbed Nathan, then began trying to leave. Logan and the others struggled to get away because they had been blinded to the Truth and no longer knew their family and friends. They were yelling saying, "Let us go! What are you doing to us? Let us go!"

Caleb and the others wouldn't let them go. Those who weren't holding them made a circle around them and moved on. The demons were hissing and yelling at Caleb and the others. They were spitting and vomiting at them. Others were leaping at them and throwing fire balls. As the demons leapt at them, the men wielded their Spirit Swords and sliced the demons in half. The demons crawled inside the people of the dome to attack. Caleb saw this and took his Sword and held it above his head making circles in the air. As he did a bright white light formed above them. He brought the Sword down quickly, the sword pointing out at the people. Just then a light shot out in beams and hit everyone in the Black Dome and blinded them including the demons.

The shadow demons were in pain and shouting out blasphemies. Caleb took his brother and threw him over his shoulder and started carrying him.

The others did the same. All the while, the crying and yelling of the demons grew louder and louder as they approached the Dome wall.

When they finally reached the wall of the Dome, Eli'Zur took his Spirit Sword and struck the wall. Then Peter took Nathan and pushed him through the opening, then struck the wall with his Sword and jumped through.

Then Eli'Zur struck the wall again, pushed Seth through and then he went through. When Caleb approached the wall, he struck it with his Sword and started to push Logan through. Suddenly a demon grabbed his foot struggling to keep Logan in the Dome. Caleb quickly took his Sword and cut off the demon's arm, then pushed Logan through the opening. As he went through the demon's arm that was still attached to his leg disintegrated. Then Caleb and the other men struck the wall and went through.

Once on the other side, Logan, Seth and Nathan regained consciousness. Logan knew his brother, but along with Seth and Nathan, had no memory of being in the Dome. They all joined in a circle and heart-linked with the Timeless-One. Then they all joined in with Caleb and sang a song of thanksgiving.

"Great and powerful are,
You Timeless-One.
You deliver us
And never tire
Holy and worthy of praise
We shout for joy
You hear us
We give you the glory."

Caleb hugged and kissed his brother as Logan cried, "Caleb, I'm sorry…"

Caleb put his hand up and interrupted Logan saying, "Let's go home."

To be continued…

3
THE STORY

*"For God so loved the world
that He gave His only begotten
Son, that whoever believes in Him should not perish but have
everlasting life."*

John 3:16

"Caleb, Caleb, Caleb!" yelled the children as they ran up to Caleb, the High Priest. He sat on a large rock by the stream reading the Holy Verses.

Caleb jumped to his feet alarmed, "What's wrong? Tell me! What's wrong?"

"Tell us a story," said a child. "Please, please," they begged.

"A story? "asked Caleb. "You guys scared me. I thought something was wrong."

"Scared? You don't get scared." said another child. "Come on, come on, please?" they yelled.

"Alright, alright, I'll tell you a story." said Caleb laughing.

"Yeah, yeah!" yelled the children.

"But I was worried," Caleb said under his breath. "Gather around everyone and sit down." He sat back down on the rock.

"What kind of story are you going to tell?" asked a little girl.

"Well Leanne, I don't know. What do you think?" replied Caleb.

"Not a scary one, okay?" said another little girl.

Caleb picked up the little girl and sat her on his lap and said laughing, "Okay Danielle, not a scary one." Caleb smiled and put his hand up to his chin and acted like he was in deep thought. Then all of a sudden, he threw his hand up and pointed to the sky and yelled, "I got it!" All the children jumped in fright.

"That wasn't funny!' said Kim as she crossed her arms in disapproval.

"Yes, it was." said Michael laughing.

All right let's get started." said Caleb.

"Wait, wait for us!" yelled two more children running up to hear Caleb's story. "Come on Phillip. Kayla come, sit right here." The children sat there with their eyes wide-open ready for the story, because they know Caleb tells great stories.

"Is everyone ready?" Caleb asked.

"Yes, yes." all the children yelled together.

"Here we go." Caleb said starting the story. "In a time yet to come; in a land not yet discovered; on an ancient world; in an unknown galaxy, there were two Kingdoms, the one in the north ruled by King Ado Nai, and the one in the south ruled by King Apollyon. Now King Ado Nai is loved by all that dwell in his Kingdom. No one says an unkind word about him, and all serve with gladness.

In addition, King Ado Nai serves his people with loving kindness. However, King Apollyon is a little different. He is hated by all. Those who dwell in his Kingdom serve him in slavery and bondage and with many stripes on their backs. King Apollyon is known as the "King of Pain."

"King Ado Nai and King Apollyon are great enemies. They have been enemies since way before time began. The two kings have had many battles. King Apollyon has never won a battle. At one time King Apollyon served in King Ado Nai's court. That is, until he thought he should be king. Then one day, he rebelled and revolted against King Ado Nai, and one third of the kingdom followed Apollyon in his revolt. There was a great war, and the Sons of Ado Nai which are the king's army removed Apollyon and his followers from the kingdom. So Apollyon built his own kingdom. From that point, King Ado Nai and King Apollyon have been enemies."

"But why did Apollyon not like King Ado Nai?" asked a young boy. "No one really knows Levi. Maybe he thought he could be a better king," answered Caleb.

"Apollyon is mean! I don't like him!" said a little girl.

"Yes, he is Elizabeth," Caleb said smiling. "Do you want me to go on?" asked Caleb.

"Yes, yes! Please!" yell all the children.

"Alright, let's see," Caleb continues his story. "Oh, yes. So, one day two young girls came before King Ado Nai in tears. 'What are your names?' King Ado Nai asked.

"The older of the two answered saying, 'My name is Sarah, and this is Kay.' 'What is it that you need?' asked King Ado Nai.

"'It's our brothers, Wayne and Leslie.' cried Sarah.

"'What about your brothers?' asked The King.

'They have been taken Your Majesty!' said Kay. 'Taken by whom? Who has taken your brothers?' King Ado Nai demanded. 'By King Apollyon!' cried Sarah. 'The Fallen Ones came in the night and took them out of their beds while we slept!' said Kay. 'We've got to get them back! Please help!' cried Sarah while wiping her eyes.

"King Ado Nai felt great compassion for the girls. He stepped down off his throne and got on his knees in front of the girls. He put his hands on their shoulders, looked in their eyes, and said, 'We will get them back. Don't worry. You have my word.' Then he sent them home."

"That's so sad," said one of the little girls sitting by Caleb.

"Don't cry Rae," said Caleb as he smiled at the children. "Should I stop now?"

"No! No, don't stop! Keep going!" yelled the children.

So, Caleb began again saying, "King Ado Nai sent for his son Emmanuel. Emmanuel came and stood before King Ado Nai and said, 'Yes, Most Holy One, how may I serve you this day?' King Ado Nai answered saying, 'Apollyon has taken two young boys. We must get them back.' 'If we must get them back, then we will get them back…whatever it takes,' said Emmanuel.

"Emmanuel gathered the Sons of Ado Nai together and set out for King Apollyon's Kingdom. When they arrived, King Apollyon's army The Fallen Ones met them at the gate. King Apollyon was ready for them. He knew King Ado Nai wouldn't let this go. The Commander of King Apollyon's army spoke saying, 'Emmanuel! King Apollyon has a message for you!'

"'Speak, for these words may be your last! What is the message?' replied Emmanuel. The Commander answered saying,

'Strong words for a defeated man. If you try to take these boys, if you touch one soldier…the boys are dead!' The Commander and the Fallen Ones then started laughing their evil laugh.

Emmanuel knew this day would come, the day when staffs and swords would not win the war. He knew what he had to do."

Caleb stood to his feet and stretched his arms up and yawned and said, "I'll finish the story tomorrow. Okay?"

The children jumped to their feet and yelled saying, "No! You've got to finish! Please!"

Then one girl pulled on Caleb's arm. Caleb looked down at her and she said, "Please finish the story, Caleb."

"Are you sure you want me to finish it Katie?" asked Caleb.

Katie and her brother Will nod their heads. All the children pleaded saying, "Please."

"Okay, okay. I'll finish." Caleb said laughing. He sat back down and continued the story.

"Emmanuel told the Commander that he wanted to see King Apollyon. The Commander said, 'Follow me!'

"'One second.' said Emmanuel. Emmanuel turned and spoke to his Captain saying, 'Go to my Father and tell him that I must do what we have talked about for so long. The day has come. Now go and don't delay.' Emmanuel turned back around and said to the Commander, 'Let's go.'

"The Commander and the Fallen Ones led Emmanuel bound with chains to King Apollyon's throne room. When King Apollyon saw Emmanuel walk through the doors, he was puzzled but pleased. As Emmanuel stood before Apollyon, all the court was silent. Apollyon leaned forward on his throne and said, 'I never thought I would see you standing in my court room.

But I am pleased.' Leaning back in his throne Apollyon says, 'Now what can I do for you this day Emmanuel?'

"Emmanuel took two steps forward and said, 'I have a deal for you.'

"'What kind of deal?' questioned Apollyon.

"Emmanuel took two more steps toward Apollyon and said, 'Take me instead, my life for the children's.'

"'What did you say?' asked Apollyon in disbelief.

"'Take my life and let the boys go free.' replied Emmanuel. 'This must be a joke!' said Apollyon.

"'No joke.' said Emmanuel.

"Apollyon stood to his feet in disbelief, 'You are willing to give up your life for these brats?'

"'Yes, I Am.' replied Emmanuel. King Apollyon grinned and stepped down off his throne. He clasped his hands behind his back and walked slowly toward Emmanuel and stopped right in front of him. Looking Emmanuel straight in the eyes and said softly, almost in a whisper, 'Oh, yes, it's a deal. It is most definitely a deal.' Still looking Emmanuel in the eyes Apollyon raised his right hand and said in a deep growling voice to the Fallen Ones in the court room, 'Take him!'

"'Are you guy's alright?' asked Caleb. The children wiped their eyes and said, "Yes, we're okay. Please keep going." "Okay, I'll keep going." replied Caleb.

Caleb continued saying, "As they released Wayne and Leslie the Fallen Ones took Emmanuel out into the courtyard. They led him to the center of the yard where there stood a tall wooden pole with a metal ring on top.

They tied his hands together, took the other end of the rope, threw it through the ring on top of the pole, and pulled it until Emmanuel's feet were barely touching the ground. Then the Fallen Ones began beating Emmanuel with a whip made of leather and steel.

They beat him until his flesh was hanging off him. He started having a hard time breathing. King Apollyon came out and stood before Emmanuel.

He pulled out his sword, held it to Emmanuel's throat, and said, 'Well, Son of Ado Nai, the time has come. I have waited centuries for this moment. Sweat is the smell of your blood. Do you have any last words?'

"Emmanuel lifted his head, looked Apollyon straight in the eye, took a deep breath, and said, 'You lose!'

'I don't think so,' replied Apollyon. At that he took his sword and thrust it into Emmanuel's heart. Emmanuel's blood poured out of him. Then suddenly a violent wind blew across the Kingdom, spreading Emmanuel's blood everywhere. Whoever was touched by Emmanuel's blood was made free. Everyone in King Apollyon's kingdom was touched by the blood of Emmanuel and they ran out of Apollyon's kingdom. Apollyon and the Fallen Ones could not stop them.

"Apollyon's kingdom fell that day, by his own sword. The people of his kingdom were freed, and Wayne and Leslie were reunited with their sisters. So many other families were also reunited that day.

"Now, before you say anything, Emmanuel did not remain dead. King Ado Nai had the power to give life back to his son. So, King Ado Nai and Emmanuel were reunited. And so, they all lived happily ever after, the end."

All the children stood to their feet and cheered. They clapped their hands and hugged Caleb. Then one of Caleb's ministers came up to him and said, "Caleb, Eli'Zur needs to see you. There's trouble in the Far Land."

"Thank you, Christopher, tell him I'll be right there."

To be continued...

4
THE FIRE

"I indeed baptize you with water
unto repentance, but He who is coming after me is mightier than I
whose sandals I am not worthy to carry. He will baptize you with the
Holy Spirit and fire."

Acts 2:1-4

As they stood in the Temple Yard, Eli'Zur told Caleb about the trouble in the Far Land saying, "Servant has gathered the witches of the Valley. They have begun to conjure." "Who is Servant, and why are the witches conjuring?" asked Caleb. "Servant," Eli'Zur explains, "was Mr. Wizard's apprentice, and he is a very evil man. He calls on the Dragon for power as well as the littlest of gods. He believes the littlest of gods has given him the power to live forever and rule this earth and the astral plane." Eli'Zur paused and with a shutter continued, "Caleb, he performs the bloody sacrifice. And he plans to get revenge for the death of his master. He plans to use the witches to help him."

"Why are the witches conjuring, they know their spells cannot come on High Rock?" asked Caleb.

"I heard the Dark Eyes talking that the witches are going to invoke the evilest of demons to go into the Far Land. They plan to torment the people that dwell there causing disease and possession of the mind and body." replied Eli'Zur.

Then, Caleb said in anger, "We must stop Servant and his witches! Servant must die!"

Just as he finished that sentence, a fire came down from Heaven in the form of a dove and hovered right in front of Caleb's face. Then, from within the fiery dove came the voice of the Timeless-One saying, "Caleb... High Priest. Be angry, but do not sin."

Caleb and Eli'Zur were paralyzed. They could not shade their eyes, and they could not fall to their knees. The Timeless-One continued speaking saying, "Servant shall not die. Take the fire to him. Caleb, take Servant the fire." Then the dove of fire came at Caleb and slammed into his chest. For a moment, Caleb looked like a pillar of fire. Yet his flesh did not burn. When the fire faded from Caleb's body, he stood motionless with tears running down his face.

Eli'Zur fell to his knees in worship to the Timeless-One. Caleb's eyes became like flames of fire, and his heart glowed in his chest. His spirit had been renewed. The Timeless-One had put in Caleb a new heart, a heart of fire, full of desire to do the will of the Timeless-One.

"Caleb," said Eli'Zur excitedly. "The Timeless-One, He spoke to you! I should not have been here! My ears should not have heard! My eyes should not have seen!"

Caleb interrupted and put his hands on Eli' Zur's shoulders saying, "Eli'Zur, calm down. It is all right. You were meant to see, you needed to hear. Come, Servant needs us. He is in need of the Fire."

Caleb and Eli'Zur called on Logan, Caleb's brother, along with Christopher, Caleb's Chief Minister to join them on their journey to the Far Land. Logan is about six-foot tall, short black hair and muscular and loves to wrestle. Christopher is very tall and lanky; he has shoulder length messy hair with a few strays on his chin, he cannot tolerate people who defy the Timeless-One. The next day they gathered their supplies and set out for the Far Land. As soon as they left High Rock, they knew the witches were conjuring. It was noonday, but outside High Rock, it looked as though it was dusk. The sky had a green tint and, the trees had no leaves and looked like shadows. The air was still and stale. No birds were singing, and no animal of any kind was in sight. The men did not say anything for a long time.

Logan broke the silence by saying, "I hear Servant is a hundred times wicked than Mr. Wizard was."

"He's a wimp," said Christopher. They all stopped walking and looked at Christopher. "What?" asked Christopher. They said nothing and just looked at him. "Does he worship the Timeless-One?" asked Christopher.

"No! Then he's a wimp." answered Christopher.

Caleb shook his head with a little grin, and said, "Let's go."

As they walked, they came upon a small village, but still no animals. The people there could not speak, since their mouths had been sealed shut by the witches' magic. The witches' spell had caused boils and open sores to come upon the people. In great pain, they would scrape their bodies with glass and rocks. Those not afflicted by the boils were possessed by evil spirits and were jumping into fire. They were in such pain and agony.

"Caleb," Eli'Zur said, "What are we going to do?"

Caleb did not say anything. Logan and Christopher immediately started heart-linking with the Timeless-One.

Then, with a loud noise the voice of the Timeless-One was heard saying, "Caleb, High Priest, give the people the Fire."

Eli'Zur lifted his hands up, threw his head back, and began to heart-link. Caleb put his hands to his chest that glowed with the Fire of the Timeless-One and looked to the Heavens. Then with a loud voice he yelled, "Receive!" As he yelled, he thrust his hands out straight, when he did, fire shooting out from them, covered the entire village and everyone in it; covering spirits and purifying hearts. The demons that the witches had sent fled the people and the village in a loud and screeching noise. The demons were black as the blackest coal. None were over a foot tall, but all had razor sharp teeth and claws. The demons were forced out of the people's ears, noses and mouths as they dug their claws into the people's flesh trying to hold on. The force of the Fire was too great and powerful for the witch's demons. The demons tried to escape, but one by one they were pulled down into the earth, into the bottomless pit for punishment.

Instantly the people were transformed from tormented, possessed and lost souls into healed, Fire filled and rescued souls. Once they were in darkness, now in the Light of the Timeless-One. The people once had eyes of black evil, and now eyes of pure light and love. The boils and soars were instantly healed as were their minds. All the people fell to their knees and rejoiced and worshipped the Timeless-One.

Servant watched all this happen through his crystal ball, and he was outraged. He commanded the witches who stood around the magic circle to attack Caleb and his men. The High Priestess held her dagger high above her and drew an inverted pentagram in the air.

As she did, she began chanting a spell saying, "Oh, great Cernunnos, and all powerful Horned One! I conjure thee to come and receive the breath of Caleb the Priest and his loathsome men! His life is yours, come and feast. Mighty Cernunnos, so mote it be!"

The Timeless-One opened Caleb and his men's ears so they could hear the High Priestess chant her spell. When the Priestess finished her spell, a hideous looking demon emerged from within the pentagram with a loud hissing sound and a green flame behind it. It had six-foot-long bat-like wings, claws like that of eagles and a head like a lion. Fire spewed from its mouth as it flew with great speed heading straight for Caleb. Eli'Zur, Logan and Christopher started heart-linking with the Timeless-One. Caleb stretched his left hand toward heaven and his right hand he stretched toward the direction of the witches, who were still far off. While he waited on the Timeless-One, Caleb grew angrier with a righteous anger that could not be extinguished. He began sweating and his chest and arms began to tremble. His eyes became as flames of fire as he looked in the direction of the witches. After three minutes, a white light came down out of Heaven like lightening and landed on Caleb's head. It went through his body and shot out his hand like a laser. It passed through the flying demon as though it was not there, the demon exploded with a screech. The light continued straight to the dagger the High Priestess held in the air. The light moved down her arm and into her body and exploded. When she exploded, the light shot out from her and went into the other witches, and then they burst into flames, and were no more.

Servants' crystal ball started glowing intensely bright, and then he heard a voice. The voice was that of Caleb saying, "Servant, I am coming. And the Fire is with me."

Servant yelled and pulled at his hair in anger. Suddenly his crystal ball shattered into a million pieces. Servant roared in his anger, "Caleb must die! I must kill Caleb! DO YOU HEAR ME CALEB? I'M GOING TO KILL YOU!"

Before Caleb and the men left, Caleb led the people of the village in a song of praise and thanksgiving to the Timeless-One.

> "Oh Timeless-One,
> We felt the Fire of your love,
> We can smell the incense,
> Of your glory.
> We thank you for your deliverance,
> We thank you for your love,
> We give you thanks Mighty One,
> We give you thanks and lift you up."

They left the village and continued on to the Far Land. The closer they got, the darker it got. Servant also left his dwelling place, headed for the Far Land. He gathered three of the wickedest magicians of the black arts he knew. Servant planned to meet Caleb and his men at the Far Land, and that is where he planned to kill him.

The next day Caleb and his men arrived at the edge of the Far Land. They stood on hill looking over the darkened valley. Caleb pointed at a city far off in the distance and said, "There, that is where we will meet Servant."

"What? What did you say? Meet who? You didn't say Servant!" said Christopher very excitedly.

"The Timeless-One has revealed to my spirit that Servant will be there waiting for us." replied Caleb.

"Thanks for sharing." Christopher said under his breath. The city sat in a valley surrounded by four mountains. One mountain was at the north, and one was at the south. Another was at the east, and the last was at the west. Caleb and his men were coming in from the west, and Servant and his men came in from the east.

When Caleb and his men arrived at the city, they saw that all the people appeared to be in a state of intoxication. However, upon closer observation, the men realized they were demon tormented. Some were having severe seizures; others were engaging in orgies and even rape. Others were desecrating the Temple with child sacrifices. Logan, Eli'Zur and Christopher began heart-linking with the Timeless-One. Caleb lifted his hands to the heavens and said with a loud voice, "Oh, Timeless-One show your power and glory now!" Then Caleb brought his hands down and pressed them to his chest and shouted with the voice of authority, "In the name of the Timeless-One, release these people! Feel the Fire, taste the Flame of the glory of All Mighty God!" Then he thrust his hands out from his chest toward the city. Again, fire erupted from his hands and swept through the city like a whirlwind, touching everybody and everything, and purifying all.

The demons hurled themselves from the mouths of the people with a shriek. As they did the people fell to the ground unconscious. The demons had the body of a frog with a serpent for a tail. They too had razor sharp teeth and claws, with black slime dripping from them. They tried to escape but were consumed by the Fire. As the Fire covered them, they became a pillar of flame that lasted about three seconds and was gone with a popping sound. Not even their ashes were left behind. Caleb and his men let the people lay where they were, for there were so many.

"What's the plan Caleb?" asked Logan.

"Yeah, how are we going to kill Servant?" added Christopher.

"We are not going to kill Servant." said Eli'Zur.

"What!?" asked Christopher. "The Timeless-One has said Servant shall not die. I am to give him the Fire." explained Caleb.

"After all he has done, we're going to let him live?" asked Christopher.

"Just as the Timeless-One has said." answered Caleb. Christopher was not happy, but trusted Caleb.

"He's here." said Caleb. Eli'Zur, Logan and Christopher looked off in the distance at the city square and there stood Servant and the three magicians.

Caleb and his men remained there as Servant and the three magicians approached them with great anger.

Servant stopped right in front of Caleb and immediately said, "Vengeance is mine Priest! You killed my master, now I'm going to kill you!"

"Wimp." said Christopher tauntingly. One of the three magicians threw a green ball of fire at Christopher; Logan grabbed his spirit sword and hit the ball of fire, sending it back to the magician knocking him down on the ground.

Caleb lifted his hand to Logan and Christopher and Servant did the same to his men. Then Caleb said, "Before you kill me, I need to give you something."

"And what might that be?" asked Servant. "Just a gift from someone you haven't met yet." replied Caleb.

Logan, Eli'Zur, and Christopher began heart-linking with the Timeless-One. "What are they doing?" demanded Servant. Caleb did not answer but lifted his hands toward the heavens.

"Now what are YOU doing?" asked Servant angrily. Just then, the ground and the mountains started shaking. The three magicians fled in fear and left Servant by himself. Then the sky turned red, and it started thundering. Servant nervously asked, "What's going on? What's happening?"

Caleb calmly said, "Servant, take the gift. The Fire is yours." Then Caleb thrust his hands forward at Servant.

Fire flew out of his hands and engulfed Servant. Before the three magicians got out of the city, the Fire reached them, and they fell down dead. A black shadow in the form of a winged serpent rose out of the back of Servant.

As this shadow demon tried to fly off Christopher took his Spirit sword hurled it at the beast. It penetrated the demon through the chest, and it disappeared with loud eerie screech. Servant threw his hands toward Heaven and began crying. For the first time in his life he felt shame and guilt. He knew at that second, he had been deceived all his life. Every person he had hurt rushed through his mind, as did every life he had taken. Then he fell to his knees and covered his face with his hands. Caleb bent down, put his hands on Servants shoulders, and said, "Take the gift."

Servant replied saying, "I'm not worthy. I'm not worthy of such a gift." Servant cried bitterly.

"The Timeless-One has chosen you. None of us is worthy. Not one. Take the gift, the Fire is yours." said Caleb.

"I accept, I accept." cried Servant.

Then a light came down from heaven and covered Servant, and out of the light came the voice of the Timeless-One thundering, "Now, Servant you are mine. Breathe the Fire and live."

Servant looked up with glow on his face and eyes full of light.

Caleb helped Servant to his feet and said, "Come, with us back to High Rock. You can live there. We would love to have you."

"Thank you, but I must stay here in the city and help the people of the Far Land. I owe them." replied Servant.

"Very well," said Caleb, "never let go of the Fire. Now you must heart-link daily to the Timeless-One, which will keep the Fire burning. And do come to High Rock and visit."

"Thank you I will." said Servant. Caleb hugged Servant.

Christopher walked up to Servant, said, "You're no wimp, man," and gave him thumbs up.

Caleb, Logan and Christopher went back to High Rock and told everyone about their adventure.

To be continued…

5
THE CONTEST

"Praise the Lord
Praise God in His sanctuary
Praise Him in His mighty firmament
Praise Him for His mighty acts
Praise Him according to His
excellent greatness
Praise Him with the sound or the
trumpet
Praise Him with the lute and harp!
Praise Him with the timbrel and
dance
Praise Him with stringed instruments
and flutes
Praise Him with loud cymbals;
Praise Him with clashing cymbals
Let everything that hath breath
Praise the Lord
Praise the Lord."

Psalm 150

Caleb sat playing the stringed instrument with the other musicians of High Rock. Caleb is not only the High Priest, but he is also Chief Musician and Worship Leader as well.

Once a day, at noon, the people of High Rock gather at the Temple Yard for a time of praise and worship to the Timeless-One. There is singing, dancing and loud music, all done in the Spirit, praising the Timeless-One for his goodness. This is a time of celebration and worship, and a time for honoring and shouting praises to the Timeless-One. This is a very sacred and joyous time.

Now while they were all in full worship Caleb suddenly stopped playing and motioned for the others to do the same. All the people stopped singing and dancing and put their hands down from worshipping. They began looking around wondering what was wrong. Then Caleb said, "Do you smell that?"

"What *is* that smell?" asked one of the musicians.

Caleb put down his stringed instrument and walked to the gates of High Rock located east of the Temple Yard. The musicians and some of the people followed him. When Caleb approached the gate, there on the other side stood three hideous looking demons. All three stood about three feet tall. Two of them did not speak for they had no mouths. Where their mouths would have been were what looked like flutes sticking out from their face. They had bodies of hairless oversized rats, and their heads were that of a wounded man. They had no eyes, just dark black holes. The third demon had the body of a hairless red skin monkey. It had a head of a large frog, and the tail of a serpent. This one did speak. He grabbed the closed gate and jumped up and down violently, and with an evil, slurring voice he said, "Umm, yess-yess, Ca-lube, Hi-eye Pries-sty. I-eye coom froom theee great-eye darkest mus-si-cianz Lamen-ta-shoon."

Caleb crossed his arms, and in disgust said, "What does Lamentation want?"

The demon began violently jumping up and down again. He then pulled himself to the bars. With his face against the gate he said, "Umm, your-eye mus-si-cal play-ing a-bil-li-ties hazz rea-ched Lamen-ta-shoonz ear-eyez."

"And?" asked Caleb. By this time Eli'Zur, Logan and Christopher were now standing by Caleb.

The demon fiercely shook the gate and yelled wickedly, "Yess-yess! Umm, yess-yess! Lamen-ta-shoon wantz tooy chal-leeng you-eye tooy aye batt-ely. Aye batt-ely withy instru-mentzy."

Christopher spoke up and said, "Why? What is the point of that?"

The demon climbed up the gate a little ways and said, "Oh, umm yess-yess, eef Lamen-ta-shoon winz, hee geetz, Ca-lubez string-eye instru-mentzy."

"And if I prove to be the best." said Caleb, "Lamentation must fall to his knees and worship the Timeless-One. Agreed?"

The demon yelled and jumped off the gate and did two backward flips in the air, then jumped back on the gate and pulled himself close. He cocked his head to one side and said, "Umm, yess-yess, thatz, woo-eld beee ex-cept-eabley."

"Tell Lamentation," said Caleb, "that three days pass the Day of Praise; we will meet him at the town square in New Sodom, before the rooster crows."

The demon yelled, jumped off the gate and the three ran off.

Caleb looked at Christopher and said, "Go to Wah'li'si and have her meet us in my office. Tell her, we need her."

Christopher nodded, and then left. Caleb, Logan and Eli'Zur went on to his office. As they were leaving, the people were still in the Temple Yard. Caleb stopped and smiled and said, "Do not worry, all is well."

Wah'li'si is a woman of High Rock that the Timeless-One has blessed with an extra portion of his Fire. Her singing blesses all those who hear her, and her dancing greatly pleases the Timeless-One. Her beauty is pure and she looks as though she has bathed in light. She is thirty years of age and is a leader among the women. All the young girls want to grow up to be just like her. "Desire the Timeless-One, for he will give you the Fire. Desire me, and you will always want." she would softly tell them.

When Wah'li'si arrived at Caleb's office, Eli'Zur, Logan and Christopher were already there. Caleb walked over to her and greeted her with a kiss on the cheek and said, "Thank you for coming."

"What is going on Caleb? Does it have anything to do with those little demons you were talking to?" she asked.

"Yes, it's Lamentation." replied Caleb.

"Lamentation?" questioned Wah'li'si.

"Lamentation has challenged Caleb to a battle of instruments. He's a wimp." Christopher said under his breath.

"Why would he do that?" asked Wah'li'si.

"I don't know," replied Caleb. "Maybe he feels he needs to prove something to himself, or maybe he needs to prove something to his followers. Whatever the reason, we must go. Lamentation must lose so he can win. He is lost and must be found."

Then Eli'Zur said, "Now New Sodom is a two day journey. We must leave the morning following the Day of Praise." Then Caleb led them in a heart-link to the Timeless-One, before they all went to their own homes.

Three days later, early in the morning, they all met in the Temple Yard. They leave this day for New Sodom, but before leaving, they heart-link to the Timeless-One for guidance and strength.

The people of High Rock came to see Caleb and the rest of the group off on their journey. The children hung on Caleb begging him not to go, but Caleb just smiled and told them that he had to go and would be back soon. As soon as everyone said their goodbyes, they left for the contest. They all agreed to fast until after the battle, to remain focused on the task. As they journeyed, no words were spoken for hours. Then Caleb began singing a song:

"You cause the wind to blow,
And we follow,
You cause the sun to shine,
And we run,
Ten thousand miles is just,
A step away.
Oh-we follow,
You lead,
Oh-we listen,
You speak,
Oh-we cling
You hold,
We love,
You, more and more."

As they walked, they all joined in Caleb's song of praise. As night set in they found a place to camp and rest for the night.

Logan built a fire and they all sat around it and warmed themselves. Eli'Zur spoke saying, "Tomorrow morning after we cross the next ridge, we will come to the Valley of Black Air."

"The Valley of Back Air?" said Christopher.

Eli'Zur continued, "The Valley of Black Air is ruled by the Dark Prince. Anyone who enters his valley and breathes his black air dies instantly."

"You have got to be kidding!" replied Christopher.

"All will be well Christopher." explained Caleb, "The Timeless-One has sent his angels ahead of us to protect us and keep us. He will not forsake his children. He is here. We are well."

Caleb smiled at them, and with that, they were comforted.

They all sat around the fire and were very quiet for the longest time. Wah'li'si gazed deeply into the flames. Then, lifting her hands, palms up she spoke softly into the fire saying,

> "Breathe unto me love,
> Breathe unto me life,
> Breathe unto me desire,
> Breathe unto me fire,
> Breathe unto me life."

All was still and quiet. There was such a stillness and peacefulness. The only sound was that of the fire and the crackling of the wood. A gentle breeze blew through the trees. The air had such a sweet aroma. Caleb took a deep breath, and suddenly, the wind rushed in, blowing with a great force. Bending and whipping the trees back and forth. All around Caleb's camp was this whirl wind, but inside the camp it was very calm. The flames of the campfire lifted straight up reaching ten feet tall. Then from out of the flames came the voice of the Timeless-One saying, "Woman, I see in you a passion to sing and a passion to dance; a passion to praise and a passion to always feel the Fire. Such passion and such radiance. I will bless you and give you your heart's desire."

Wah'li'si fell forward with her face to the ground. The men stood to their feet and lifted their hands, palms up. Wah'li'si sat back up and spoke into the fire once more, saying,

"Blessed art thou oh, Lord,
Blessed and Holy,
Blessed is He, who sits on the throne,
With power and glory,
Oh-a Holy Wonderment."

Then she began to sing,

"Holy Wonderment, A Mystery, oh Majesty,
Holy Wonderment,
A Mighty King, the Prince of Peace,
Holy Wonderment,
The Rock did bleed, a Savior indeed,
Holy Wonderment."

Wah'li'si stood to her feet and began dancing in the Spirit, while the men sang her song. They were all in full worship, and this lasted for about an hour. The wind grew still as did Caleb and the rest. All was quiet now. The Spirit of the Timeless-One gave each of them a full revival and a renewing of the spirit.

When morning came, they all awoke and felt energized. They gathered their things and started on their journey again. They quickly came to the hill that looked over the Valley of Black Air. The air was visible. It was black and dark green. It moved and swirled around like someone stirring two different colors of paint together.

"The only way to New Sodom is through the valley." said Caleb.

"Rub it in." said Christopher under his breath.

As they got closer to the valley, they saw a bright light at the edge. The closer they got, the brighter and larger the light got. The light did not move from its spot. When they reached the valley, and the light, they saw at once that the light was the Word of the Timeless-One.

They immediately fell to the ground, lying face down in fear and in worship. The Word smiled when He saw Caleb, then bent down and took him by the arm and helped him up.

Still smiling the Word said in almost an excited voice, "Caleb, it is I, your friend." Then, putting His hands on Caleb's shoulders, and looking into his eyes with His flaming eyes of fire said, "Do not be afraid, Caleb. I am here."

Then the Word pointed at the valley and said, "Look, I have cleared a path for you. Fear not, the Dark Prince nor can his black air touch you. Go, and complete your mission."

When he had finished speaking, He was lifted up into the Heavens. Then they saw right before their eyes a large circular tunnel made of pure white light, leading straight through the Valley of Black Air. Caleb said to the others, "Come, let us go, for the Lord is our Shelter and our Strength." As they walked through the tunnel of light, they could see on either side of them that there were thousands of mighty angels, standing side by side keeping the Dark Prince and the black air from touching them. About halfway through the tunnel Caleb and Wah'li'si led the others in another song of praise to the Timeless-One,

"You shelter your servants,
With your mighty wings,
You hide us in the,
Cleft of the Rock,
We walk in the midst,
Of your Glory,
Your spirit has given us,
A champion's heart."

When they came out the other side of the tunnel, they all lifted their hands, palms up, and held their heads back and heart-linked with the Timeless-One. They did not look back but moved forward.

As they walked on, they came upon three men bound in heavy chains. One was standing, and the other two were lying on the ground, for their chains were heavier than the one who was standing.

Caleb spoke to the one standing, "Who has done this to you?"

The man said nothing. He just stood there swaying back and forth.

Logan bent down where the other two laid and said, "Tell us, who is responsible for doing this to you."

There was no response. They just laid there on the ground and moaned.

"No one has done this to them." said Wah'li'si.

"What do you mean, no one did this to them?" asked Christopher.

"I mean they did this to themselves." replied Wah'li'si. "Look," continued Wah'li'si. "The chains have no locks, and there is no beginning and no end. Look." She then reached over to touch the chain on the one standing. When her hand came to the chain, her hand passed right through it and touched his chest. The man fell to the ground and began shaking and jerking violently.

She said, "These chains are their sins. They are bound by their own sins." Wah'li'si walked over to Caleb and said, "Give them the Fire. Only then can they be free."

Eli'Zur, Logan, Christopher and Wah'li'si started heart-linking with the Timeless-One. Caleb lifts his hands up then puts them to his chest. After one minute, he thrust his hands out toward the men. The Fire shot out from Caleb's hands and covered the men like volcanic lava. The men fell unconscious as the Fire lifts the men off the ground. The chains melted off the men and disappeared before hitting the ground.

The Fire let the men down gently onto their feet. The men immediately fell to their knees and lifted their hands in worship. They thanked the Timeless-One for releasing them from there bondage and for giving them a new spirit.

The men's chests were glowing, for their hearts were on fire. Before Caleb and the others left, he spoke to the men saying, "The Timeless-One says, you are healed. Now go, and do not look for your chains. Feel the Fire that burns in you, and never forget this day. This is your Day of Praise. Now go and show yourselves to your families."

The men left that place, rejoicing and praising the Timeless-One.

Caleb and his group went a little further and then decided to camp for the night. They sat around the campfire and talked about the day's events.

Eli'Zur spoke saying, "Tomorrow we will be at New Sodom, but to get inside the city, we must cross the River Agony."

"No way!" said Christopher in disbelief. "The River Agony? Why? Why couldn't it be the River Peace and Quiet, or The River Honeysuckle?"

"Sorry, Christopher." replied Eli'Zur. "New Sodom sits just on the other side of the river." Eli'Zur explains. "Upriver they have a temple sitting on the bank, where they perform human sacrifices to their god Thrust."

"Human sacrifice?" asked Logan.

"Yes." replied Eli'Zur. "Young children and ladies who are virgins."

"That is horrible." said Wah'li'si.

"Now, let me tell you about the river." said Eli'Zur.

"Oh, man. Here we go." said Christopher.

Eli'Zur continues, "The sacrifices are done on top of the temple, which is the highest point of the city.

They lay the person to be sacrificed on the altar of black stone. Once the person is on the altar, they become unconscious, then they are stabbed in the heart with a two edged sword. After the blood is drained from the body and put in a container, the body is thrown in the river."

Wah'li'si wiped her tears and said, "What about the river?"

"The river cries for those who have perished by the sword in the name of Thrust." Eli'Zur continues. "When we cross the river will hear the moans and cries of the river. At times it will seem unbearable, but we must get through."

Then Caleb said, "Listen, the Timeless-One is with us. He will get us through. All is well. Let's get some sleep."

When morning came, they all arose and started out once again. As they came to the edge of the river, they saw that the river was black and very still. It was completely quiet. There were hundreds of vultures, circling the river and the temple.

"Caleb, look." said Logan, pointing at a rowboat a few yards from them.

When they got to the boat Christopher said, "Oh man, there's only four oars. I guess I'll sit in the back."

Wah'li'si walked up to Christopher and punched him in the arm. "Okay, I'll row." he said rubbing his arm. Logan and Eli'Zur laughed.

Caleb walked up to Wah'li'si asked, "You didn't hurt your hand, did you?"

"Hurt her hand?" said Christopher still rubbing his arm. As soon as they got into the boat the river began moaning and wailing. At first it was soft, but the closer they got to the temple the louder it got. By the time they got to the middle of the river, the rivers' moaning and wailing was almost unbearable. The harder the men rowed the harder the waves beat against the boat, and the louder the moaning got. The boat was rocking violently.

Then Caleb stood up in the boat and threw his oar down and shouted, "That is enough!" Then he looked up and said, "Oh, Timeless-One, to you, honor, power and glory forever and ever." Then he said, "Eli'Zur, Logan, Christopher, take your spirit swords and strike the river, one by one."

So, they each did as Caleb said, Eli'Zur went first, then Logan, and last, Christopher. As soon as Christopher's sword hit the river, a pure white light shot from it and hit the shore. The light remained after Christopher pulled his sword back. "Let's go!" said Caleb as he stepped out of the boat onto the light that hovered over the river. He did not sink but walked on the light the Timeless-One provided. Wah'li'si and the others were in awe. They too stepped out of the boat and walked across the river on the light. None of them sank, because none of them doubted.

When they reached the shore, the moaning of the river stopped as did the waves. The river became still again. They all raised their hands and gave thanks to the Timeless-One for carrying them across the river.

"That was a rush, huh guys." said Christopher.

Logan smiled and shook his head and said, "Chris, you seem to always know the right thing to say at the right time."

"Thanks man." replied Christopher. They all laughed.

"What?" said Christopher.

"Come on." said Caleb. They went on up to the gates of New Sodom. When they reached the gates, they could see the town square from there. "Lamentation is already here." said Caleb.

"How do you know?" asked Wah'li'si.

Just then the demon that was at High Rock jumped down from the top of the gate.

Caleb and the others were still on the outside of the gate and the demon was on the inside. The demon jumped on the bars, cocked his head to one side, and said, "Wel-cume, Ca-lube cume-eye een."

The demon jumped off the bars and two other demons opened the gates. The demon jumped and did two flips in the air and said, "Fall-oh-eye meee." They followed the demon to the town square.

As they walked Caleb said, "Don't let the stench get to you. We won't be here long."

As they walked, the streets were filled with people, all dressed in black. The women also wore black vials over their faces. They looked beaten down, and full of sorrow, and inner pain. Wah'li'si and Caleb walked together. She looked over at Caleb and said, "I hurt so much for these people. They are so full of sadness." "It's Lamentation." replied Caleb.

When they reached the town square, a large stage had been set up in the middle. Lamentation jumped off the stage and said, "Welcome, welcome, welcome. I am so glad you could make it. This is going to be great." He had a very evil grin on his face. "Are you ready?" asked Caleb. "No formalities, no pleasantries. Just get to it, uh?" replied Lamentation. Caleb did not reply. "Okay, then, let's get to it. Shall we?" said Lamentation as he jumped back on stage. While Lamentation was talking to his musicians, Logan turned to Caleb and said, "Caleb, he's got a whole band." "So do I." replied Caleb. "What? Where?" asked Logan. "Eli'Zur, Christopher, Wah'li'si, and you, you guys are my band." answered Caleb. "What did you say? Did I hear right? We, are your band? I am not a musician! I cannot play an instrument! You have the wrong guy! **No! Hu, uh!** Sorry." said Christopher very rapidly and pacing back and forth. "Don't worry Christopher, all is well." said Caleb. "Caleb," said Christopher. "I am not a musician, and neither are these guys, except for Wah'li'si." "Don't worry." assured Caleb.

The people of New Sodom began gathering around the stage. Caleb and the others stood off to the side of the stage and watched. Lamentation's band will go first. As soon as they were ready, Lamentation walked to the edge of the stage with his stringed instrument and said in an echoing voice, "I dedicate this time to our god, Thrust! Mighty is he and all-powerful.

He drinks the blood of the pure, and then blesses our land. Thrust, we worship, and serve only you!" Then with his fist in the air, he and the crowd start chanting, *"Thrust, Thrust, Thrust!"* When they stopped, Lamentation and his band started playing.

Immediately the band went into a trance. The music was neither fast nor was it slow. As they played, formless shadows hovered over each musician for a few seconds, and then fell on them. When this happened, the people watching began to wail and fall to the ground, as if they were in pain. They cried out and pulled at their hair as Lamentation played on. It seemed every note he played sent more pain into the people, and some were throwing dirt and ash on their heads and covering their ears. The people had no control over their own bodies as they went into what looked like seizures. Blood began dripping from Lamentation and his bands' ears, and eyes. They never moved, and never took a step while they played. They just stood there as if under a magical spell. The shadows that fell on them were moving in and out of their bodies, controlling every sound they made. The strings on their instruments became like flames of fire but did not burn them.

Wah'li'si turned to Caleb and said, "He must stop! The people . . . . look at the people!"

Just then Lamentation stopped. The people slowly calmed down and grew quiet. It was now Caleb's turn.

Caleb turned to Logan and the rest and said, "Let's do it."

"Uh, Caleb?" said Christopher. "Did you forget something? We are *not* musicians. Even if we were, we have no instruments. Caleb, I'm serious man, I can't play anything. Tapping my foot is problem. Come on, don't make me do this."

"Don't worry Christopher, all is well. Come on." replied Caleb.

They all went up on stage, and Caleb turned his back to the crowd facing Eli'Zur and the rest, and then said, "Take your spirit swords in your hand and lay them at your feet." They all did as he said.

"Now look up and give thanks to the Timeless-One for the Spirit of praise he has given to us."

They all looked up, and lifted their hands and gave thanks, and then they all praised the name of the Timeless-One. As they were in prayer, a pure white light came down on each of them.

Then the voice of the Timeless-One came thundering out of heaven for all to hear saying, "Sing a new song to Me, and play skillfully with a loud noise. This is now a house of power, and a house of praise, a house of prayer. Worship and be glad, you have already won."

The people fell face down on the ground, and even Lamentation could not remain standing after hearing the voice of the Timeless-One. The demons fled the city with a loud screech. Christopher and the others brought their hands down and looked to see that their swords were no longer there. The Timeless-One had replaced their swords with instruments. To Logan and Eli'Zur He gave stringed instruments, and to Christopher He gave drums to play. To Wah'li'si He gave a tambourine. Caleb brought his own stringed instrument. They all took their instruments in their hands, and Christopher sat behind the drums, then Caleb said, "Let's worship."

Christopher started with a moderate drumbeat, then Wah'li'si started clapping her hands in rhythm. Then the other band members joined her in clapping.

Soon the people started clapping with them. Caleb started strumming his stringed instrument, while Logan and Eli'Zur followed his lead. Wah'li'si Started dancing in the Spirit, and then broke out in a song:

<blockquote>
"Lift up your voices,
Lift up your hands,
Lift up your hearts,
Oh, let's dance.
Feel, feel the Spirit,
Feel, feel the Fire,
Feel, feel the music,
Oh, take the Power.
Come, come Holy Spirit,
Come into this house,
Come, come Holy Spirit,
Come into Your house."
(Repeat)
</blockquote>

As they sang and played, the Spirit of the Timeless-One came down from Heaven in the form of a thousand fiery doves. The doves flew into the crowd and throughout New Sodom renewing hearts and touching souls. The whole city was now in full worship to the Timeless-One. A fiery dove landed on Lamentation, he instantly fell to the ground in tears and in worship to the Timeless-One.

A full hour had gone by when they stopped playing. The city was still in worship as Caleb walked over to Lamentation and helped him up to his feet. Lamentation hugged Caleb and said, "Thank you for bringing the Timeless-One with you."

Lamentation handed Caleb his instrument and said, "Take this, my time for mourning is over."

When Caleb took it, it crumbled and turned to dust and fell through his fingers to the ground. Then Caleb took his own instrument, handed it to Lamentation, and said, "You are no longer Lamentation. You are now known as Ovation. Take this and Praise the Timeless-One."

Ovation fell to his knees, held the instrument above his head, and wept. New Sodom was saved that day.

The instruments turned back into their Spirit Swords. So, Caleb, Eli'Zur, Logan, Christopher and Wah'li'si went back to High Rock and told everyone about their adventure.

"It was awesome." said Christopher.

To be continued...

6
THE SOUND OF SILENCE

"I am not ashamed of the gospel, because it is the power of God for the salvation of everyone who believes: first the Jew then the Gentile. For in the gospel a righteousness from God is revealed, a righteousness that is by faith from first to last, just as it is written: 'The righteous will live by faith.'"

Romans 1:16, 17)

"Yes, Michael? What is their condition?" asked the Timeless One.

"They are no more," said Michael the Archangel.

"They are not dead, for they are not in my presence," replied the Timeless One.

"No, Most High they are not dead," said Michael. "They are alive, but they do not eat, nor do they drink. They do not walk, nor do they lie down. They do not talk, nor do they sing. They do not sleep but they are not awake. Their hearts do beat but they cannot move. Their magic has put them in a wall-less and motionless prison. They are frozen in time. The nation A'Mer has destroyed itself in civil war. They forgot you, My Lord.

They turned to self-gratification and evil desires. They turned to witchcraft and magic. Then hate for their fellow countrymen rose. They lost love and gained skepticism."

"Tell Me, Michael, what happened," said the Timeless One.

"I know you know, Most High. But I know you want to hear it from me. A'Mer was divided. The witches are to the north, and the black magicians to the south. To the west are the Alchemist and false prophets, and to the east the worshippers of the little gods. Pride as well as spells filled the air. The littlest of gods ran rampant. All the sects tried to prove more powerful than the rest. Spells never ceased being cast.

"Then one day the littlest of gods tricked all A'Mer. He gave them all the same spell to cast on each other, at the same time. The result, they are frozen but conscious. They can see and hear but can't move or talk. If they would have not forgotten you..."

"They had no one there to tell them of Me," said the Timeless One.

Then the Son said, "There is one we can send." The sound of silence fell over heaven as the Son stood and walked to the edge of heaven.

As Caleb was heart-linking with the Timeless One the Lord spoke to him saying, "Caleb, my faithful servant, come up here so that I may speak to you face to face." Immediately, Caleb was in heaven. Just before he was taken, Eli'Zur had walked in the temple and saw Caleb heart-linking and saw him disappear.

Caleb appeared at the edge of heaven where the Son was standing. When Caleb saw the Son, he fell as dead at His feet. The Son reached down and helped Caleb to his feet. The Son gave Caleb a big smile and hugged him. When the Son let go of him, Caleb fell at his feet in worship saying, "Holy, oh holy, oh holy!" The Son reached down and touched Caleb's shoulder and said, "Caleb, its ok. Stand to your feet."

"Caleb stood up slowly. "Did I die?"

"You died many years ago, but you're not dead," replied the Son.

"This heaven?" asked Caleb.

"Yes, we are at the edge of heaven," replied the Son.

"Caleb," said the Son. "I brought you up here because you have been so faithful. Whatever I ask of you, you do, without question. You do not doubt. You have a pure, clean heart."

"Lord," said Caleb. "I don't deserve these words."

"Yes, you do Caleb," said the Son. "You have brought many into the family."

"Lord," replied Caleb. "It is your Spirit in me that has allowed me to do these deeds."

"It is your willingness and your servant's heart. It is your love for Me and your love for man's soul that allows My Spirit to work in you," replied the Son.

"Lord, your words mean everything to me. Your words are life. Without your words my heart would stop, and my breath would cease. You are my God. I live for You, and I will die for You," said Caleb.

The Son reached over and hugged Caleb and said, "I know you would Caleb. I know."

Caleb fell to the ground again in worship saying, "Holy! Oh, holy! Oh, holy!"

The Son knelt down in front of Caleb and said, "We need you to do something for us." Just as the Son finished speaking a lion charged up to Him and knocked Him over licking and wanting to play.

Caleb jumped to his feet and began run when he heard the Son, he turned and looked to see the son laughing.

The Son laughed and said to the lion, "Not now, not now. We'll play later." He got up and said to Caleb, "Come, walk with me." As they walked the lion walked with them.

"Caleb," said the Son. "The nation A'Mer is in trouble. It lies on the other side of the earth from High Rock. They have forgotten Me. The littlest of gods has poisoned their minds. They are a very wicked people. Right now, they have cursed themselves with an awful curse. You are the only on earth that can save them from destruction."

"Lord, how will I get there? What of the language, Lord," said Caleb.

"The people will hear and understand your words," replied the Son. "Michael will take you, Caleb."

They stopped walking and faced each other. The lion began rubbing against the Son's legs. The Son continues, "The people of A'Mer are frozen in time. They can't speak or move, none of them. They are like statues."

"How can I help them?" asked Caleb.

"I am not frozen in time. I am not subject to time. Time is subject to Me. I will send you to A'Mer three days prior to the curse," said the Son.

"I'm going to travel back in time?" asked Caleb.

"Yes, just as John from the Holy verses you read traveled into the future. You shall travel back in time. You will keep them from destructions," replied the Son.

As they stood there talking, Moses, David and Paul walked up to them. "Good. You made it," said the Son.

"Caleb, I would like for you to meet some friends." Walking behind them and putting his hands on their shoulders one by one he said, "This is Moses."

"Be strong and courageous Caleb. You're never alone. Here," Moses handed Caleb a staff. "Take this. If you need to use it," said Moses.

"And this is David," said the Son. "Always sing a new song. Always praise the Lord with all your soul. Caleb, the eyes of the Lord are upon you," said David.

"And this is Paul," said the Son. "Keep fighting the good fight. Finish the race – keep the faith," said Paul. "Your words will never leave me. Thank you very, very much," said Caleb.

Moses, David and Paul walked on, and then the Son said to Caleb, "I'm going to give you a gift before you go." He reached over and put His left hand on top of Caleb's head and put his right hand on his heart then said, "You now have the faith of a mustard seed and a double portion of the Spirit you already had." Then with a loud voice He said, "Caleb! High Priest of High Rock! Go and claim A'Mer for the Timeless One!"

Caleb fell at the Son's feet in worship once again saying, "Holy, oh Holy, oh Holy."

When Caleb looked up the Son was gone. He was by himself. Michael came up behind him and said, "We must go now."

Michael held his arm out and said, "Take hold of my robe." Caleb took hold of the robe. Instantly they were moving very rapidly. They weren't walking nor where they flying. But they were moving. Sound had ceased. They had left heaven but were not on earth. A rainbow of lights moved about Caleb and Michael. Caleb looking around could see Heaven's mighty warriors battling hells little gods. Heaven's warriors were binding the little gods with chains and dragging them down to hell.

Looking up, Caleb could see the floor of Heaven. Down below him he could see hell and people being tormented. He could see them screaming and crying out in pain but could not hear them. The sound of silence rang in his ears. It was almost unbearable.

Then he let go of Michael's robe and reached up and held his ears. Just as he touched his ears, Michael was gone he was standing on earth in a foreign land.

Still holding his ears, he turned around looking in all directions. Then he fell to his knees and lifted his hands toward heaven and said in a loud voice,

"Oh-Timeless One!
All power and glory belong to you.
Oh – Timeless One!
You are before time, You will be after time.
At your Word, time obeys.
Oh – guide your servant.
Lead me down the right path.
Fill your servant with every right word.
Oh – Timeless One
All power! And all glory belongs to you!"

Standing to his fee he looked around once again. He noticed to the east, to the west and to the south was barren and flat. But, to the north was a single mountain larger than High Rock. The base was several miles wide. The peak reached the clouds and could not be seen. All was still. All was silent. There was no sound at all, for the exception of the sound of his breathing. Caleb bent down and picked up the staff Moses had given him and looked up to heaven and said, "Which way?" Immediately an intensely bright white light shot out from the staff hitting the foot of the mountain. "I guess I'll go that way," he said to himself.

Caleb was walking for several hours on an open and barren land, only hearing the sound of his breath. All was silent. No birds, no plant life, no people and no wind. Then off in the distance he could see a structure. It was a man-made structure. When he came upon it, he saw it was a gate of some kind, an archway in the middle of the desert leading to nowhere. Nothing was on the side Caleb stood and nothing on the other side. It was made from a black shining metal, standing about thirteen feet tall. On top of the archway was a message written with letters he had never seen before. As he looked at the letters, the Spirit revealed to Caleb what it said. The message read:

HE WHO ENTERS SHALL BE DEVOURED BY THE MAGICK GOAT OF THE SPIRIT. YOUR BLOOD, HIS CRAVE.

Then Caleb looked toward heaven and said,

"Oh – Timeless One,
I am here, You are here.
You sent, I came
You touched my soul.
With the Holy ember
And filled my eyes with fire.
I know, You know.
My heart, your temple. Selah……. amen!"

The width of the archway was about thirteen feet, as was the depth. Caleb walked around it three times and saw nothing. So, he decided to walk through it. He got halfway through the archway and demonic voices started speaking to him saying, "Leave! Leave now or we'll kill you! Caleb, High Priest! Leave! Turn and go or we'll rip you to pieces!"

Caleb stopped, lifted his right hand and said, "Be gone! In the name of the Timeless One, go to hell!" With a loud shriek the voices left. And all was silent again.

Caleb continued through the archway.

When he stepped out on the other side, he stood in the middle of a great city. The city could not be seen from outside the archway, but once through it, there was a very populated city, but still no sound.

As Caleb stood at the opening of the archway, he looked around at the city. Every building and every home were made of the same material as the archway -- a black shiny metal. Every home and building had the same symbol on it – a circle with an inverted triangle in it. As Caleb stepped away from the archway the sound of the city filled his ears. When he turned to look at the archway, it was gone. Hanging, rather floating, in midair over where the archway was located was the same symbol made from the black metallic material.

As the Holy Spirit led, Caleb followed. He knew he was headed for the leader of the people. As he walked through town, he noticed something disturbing. None of the people had eyes. Where their eyes should be there was what looked like scales had grown over and covering the eyes. Though they did seem to be able to see clearly and did walk about the city doing their business. The people also didn't seem to care that a stranger walked among them. They just went about their business. This was a very wealthy community full of the arts and of man's wisdom.

Caleb stopped walking. Down at the end of the street he saw what looked like a temple. As he moved closer, he saw three dark figures standing at the top of a set of stairs. When he reached the temple, he stood on the sidewalk at the foot of the stairs looking up at the three men. On the building above the men were three symbols. The middle symbol was the same one that is on every structure in the city. The symbol on the left was the head of a goat. Caleb knew that it was the head of Baphomet, the goat god he encountered on the way to Mr. Wizard's dwelling place. The symbol on the right was a circle with a six-pointed star in it.

These three men had eyes but were darkened. The man standing in the middle was wearing a black hooded robe with his hands clasped in front. He had on his forehead the symbol that hung above him. The two men on either side of him had on red hooded robes. They too had their hands clasped in front of them. On their foreheads were the symbols that hung on the building above them.

The man in the middle spoke to Caleb saying, "You don't belong here! Leave now and I'll let you live!"

"I come from the other side of the earth," replied Caleb. "The Timeless One has sent me here to tell you, lest you repent of your evil ways, in just three days a great disaster will come upon the nation of A'Mer."

"My name is Therion! I know not of the Timeless One, and I believe you to be mad or a liar!" said the one in the middle. "I'll say this one more time, LEAVE and I'll let you live!"

"Only when I've completed the task set before me," replied Caleb. "The Timeless One says, 'Turn from your evil ways, know Me, and I'll know you."

Then Therion in great rage exclaimed, "Diabolos! Inimicus!" The two men standing by Therion held their hands up. From out of the symbols that hung above them fell balls of fire that they caught in their hands then hurled at Caleb. The fire balls landed on the ground by Caleb, one on his left, the other on his right. Caleb didn't move a muscle. He had no fear. Therion increased in rage. With all his anger he too threw a ball of fire at Caleb. It was heading right for his head. Just before it reached him, Caleb seized the staff Moses gave him and swung it at the ball of fire hitting it back at Therion. It flew back; explode against the temple right above Therion's head. When it hit it blew a hole in the temple where the symbol was. Pieces of the temple collapsed on the men, but they were not hurt.

"Who are you?" demanded Therion.

"My name is Caleb, High Priest of the High Rock, servant to the Timeless One. Consider this, time is short. I'll be back tomorrow," said Caleb. Caleb turned and walked out the way he came.

The archway wasn't there, but the symbol was still hovering where it was. When Caleb arrived at the symbol the archway appeared. After Caleb got through to the other side of the archway he turned around. The city was gone, but the archway remained.

Caleb walked about a half of a mile away from the city. He built a fire and heart linked with the Timeless One. Then he said unto the Timeless One,

"Hear oh Lord of All,
Hear your servant call from the past,
I'll call from a time that has already been.
To the God that always shall be.
Give me rest,
Cover me with Your mighty wings."

Then Caleb lay down and went to sleep.

At that time back in the city, Therion called a special meeting of the magicians' counsel. The counsel consisted of six men. They met in the temple around a circle that was drawn on the floor. A blue glow came from the circle and surrounded the magicians. Therion spoke saying, "We must get rid of this man tonight! He is a very dangerous man. He has strong magic. Let us cast." At that they began casting spells. They called on the God of the spirit to kill Caleb.

As Therion and the others did their evocations, demons emerged out of the floor from within the circle and flew out of the temple and out of the city. They were heading straight for Caleb. When the demons reached Caleb's camp, they found standing around it, Michael and about one hundred other angels. The demons stopped just outside the camp.

Michael saw them and said in a sarcastic and demeaning way, "Now, now little fellows, you're not thinking of doing anything silly are you? No! I didn't think so. Now, why don't you little guys go on back from where you came, or we'll send you there ourselves, ok?"

The demons turned and retreated back to the temple and jumped on Therion and the other magicians. Clawing and biting and ripping their flesh, then one of the demons said to Therion, "Caleb cannot be killed. The Spirit of the Timeless One is with him. Try to kill him yourself." Then the demons jumped back into the circle and disappeared into the floor. All the magicians fell to the floor moaning from the wounds the demons inflicted on them. Caleb never woke until morning.

Morning came and Caleb awoke, and heart linked with the Timeless One. Then he headed back to the city. About halfway back, he met a man; he was sitting on the ground humming. When the man saw Caleb approach, he jumped up and stood in front of Caleb. He crossed his arms and said, "Serpentine is my name. What is yours? Could it be the same?"

"I'm Caleb. No," he replied.

"From where do you come, far or near? I do believe I smell fear," said Serpentine.

"The Timeless One has sent me here. And the fear you smell comes from you," replied Caleb.

The man then crossed his hands six times in front of his face and said, "Can you dance to a turn? Do you know the power of the moon? Can you see your reflection in my eyes? Do you realize you're about to die?"

Caleb then said, "No. But I do know you're wasting my time." Quickly Caleb reached over and touched Serpentine on the forehead with his fingertips, then made a tight fist and said, "In the name of the Timeless One, come out of him!" Caleb pulled his fist back and in his fist, he had hold of a hideous looking demon by the neck.

The demon was about three feet in length. Caleb held him by the neck in the air. He was jerking around like a fish out of water.

Caleb looking the demon in the face said, "Go back to hell!" Caleb threw the demon to the ground. The demon passed through the ground with a shriek.

The man fell to the ground unconscious. Caleb looked up to heaven and said, "Oh Timeless One keep your protective hand over him." The Timeless One sent an angel to watch over the man and Caleb went on to the city.

When Caleb reached the city, he went straight to the temple where Therion and the counsel were waiting for him. They stood at the top of the stairs in their hooded robes. Caleb stayed on the sidewalk.

Therion said in anger and disgust, "What is it that you want?"

Then Caleb said, "All of A'Mer is headed for destruction in two days unless you repent and turn from your evil ways and worship the Timeless One."

"We worship the Magic Goat of the Spirit," said Therion. "The northern ones worship Diana and the Cernunnos. The people of the west worship Uroboros and science. Those of the east worship, well, have too many gods to mention. All of the other cities are our enemies, and you want us to come together and worship your God?"

"The One and only God, yes," replied Caleb.

"You're mad!" shouted Therion.

Then Caleb said, "Get word to the leaders of the other cities and have them meet here tomorrow. Know that the Timeless One is all powerful and is the only true God." Then Caleb took his staff and held it out and swung it around three times. As he did, an intensely bright white light shot out from the end of it hitting every symbol in the city.

When the light hit the symbols, they all melted away running down the sides of the buildings. The people of the city became terrified. Then Caleb said, "I'll be back tomorrow."

Caleb turned and left the city and went back to his campsite. On his way back he saw Serpentine waiting for him. Serpentine stopped him and said, "Thank you, thank you for your kindness."

"Thank the Timeless One and worship him," replied Caleb.

Caleb walked on to his camp and heart linked with the Timeless One. Then Caleb spoke to the Lord saying,

> "Oh, Timeless One
> Show Your great and awesome power.
> To those who are in darkness.
> Show Your Light."

Then the Timeless One gave Caleb rest and sent Michael and his angels to watch over him through the night.

Morning came. Caleb arose and heart linked with the Timeless One then went to the city. Again, he went straight to the temple. People followed him this time. The only ones standing there was Therion and the counsel.

"Where are the others?" asked Caleb.

"I sent word as you asked," replied Therion. "They did not reply. They did not come, as I knew they wouldn't."

"Then it will have to be you and your people to change your nation," said Caleb.

"We will not change, nor do we want to. Now, take your God and go!" said Therion. The crowd cheered.

"The Timeless One sent me here for a reason. You will turn. And this nation will turn because of you!" said Caleb.

Then Caleb turned and walked to the edge of the city. Therion, the counsel and the people followed. When he stopped, he turned toward the people and said, "This nation will come together and worship the Timeless One! But, first, this mountain must be removed! This mountain that you formed from hate and magic must be taken out of the way! It divides your nation, but no longer!"

Caleb turned and faced the mountain. He took his staff in his hands and held it out in front of him. Then, like a waterfall, fire fell from heaven and covered Caleb. Caleb's spirit was on fire but his flesh and clothes did not burn. Therion and the people became full of fear. They wanted to run but couldn't move. They kept saying, "What kind of magic is this?"

Caleb full of the Holy Spirit and full of faith, with a loud voice spoke to the mountain saying, "In the name of the Timeless One I command you, move! Rise and be lifted from where you were planted!"

The ground started shaking and rumbling. The people had trouble standing. Then Therion said to Caleb, "Stop this magic! Please, stop!"

Then clouds formed around the mountain and began circling it. Caleb spoke once again to the mountain saying, "In the name of the Timeless One, I command you, flee to the ocean!" Be drowned in the depths of the sea! Move! Now!" Immediately the fire surrounding him moved out from him and surrounded the base of the mountain. The ground shook violently. The people began falling. The mountain shook and growled.

Then the mountain rose slowly into the air. Rocks and boulders fell to the ground. The sound of silence filled the air. There was no sound as the mountain moved across the sky with fire blazing out from under it. Caleb stood firm with his eyes as flames of fire.

Therion and the whole city were on their knees with their faces to the ground. Caleb began laughing in the spirit as the mountain moved out of sight.

The other cities saw the mountain move but didn't know how or why, they believed their own gods had something to do with it.

Once the mountain was over the ocean, it exploded and fell into the water. Then there was sound again. Then Caleb spoke to the people, "Hear my words for they come from the Timeless-One. The Lord says 'Turn from your evil ways and come to me. There is nothing you need that I can't provide. Know me and I will know you! said the Lord'."

Then Caleb took the staff Moses gave him and drew a circle in the dirt. He lifted the staff by one end and above his head then swung it down and hit the center of the circle. The ground gave way and revealed a pit. "Oh Lord of all, open their eyes."

Smoke, fire, and a foul stench rose from the pit along with screams and wailings. The people couldn't stand to hear it so they began holding their ears. "Do you hear that?" said Caleb. "That is where the goat of the spirit dwells and that is where he wants to take you."

Then Caleb spoke to the Timeless One saying, "Oh Timeless One, open their eyes. Let them see." Then a bright white light shot down out of heaven. Like a sharp sword it cut away the flesh that covered their eyes and they were able to see. As the people looked at the pit, they could see hovering there a hideous looking demon. A body resembling a snake with wings and the head of a goat with his mouth dripping with blood – the blood of those he had devoured.

Then the goat of the spirit began his "backward" speaking said, "belaC hgih tseirP, ruoY doolb I evarc!"

The people became filled with fear, for their eyes were opened. Therion filled with fear, for their eyes were opened. Therion and the others said crying, "Save us Caleb, save us! Save us from the pit! Save us from the goat of the spirit."

Caleb looked at the demon and said while lifting his hand, "Silence!" Then the demon was unable to speak another word. Caleb then said to the people, "I cannot save you. There is only one who can save, and who can destroy. Lift your eyes and voice to the Timeless One. He can and will save you."

Then the people cried out to the Timeless One saying, "Oh Timeless One, save us, please save us."

The Spirit of the Timeless One came down from heaven like a fiery dove soaring around and passing through the hearts of everyone making them like brand new. Then with a loud shriek the goat of the spirit was sucked into the pit and sealed up with him in it. The people lifted their hands and rejoiced.

Therion fell at Caleb's feet and said "Oh Caleb please forgive me for doubting and not believing you. I'm so sorry."

Caleb reached down and helped Therion up and said, "You were blind and now you can see. You were dead, but now you are alive."

"I did evil toward you," said Therion.

"That was a long time ago," said Caleb.

Caleb gave Therion a book of the Holy Verses, and gave him the staff Moses gave him, "You and your people must take the message of the Timeless One throughout this nation. Crush the littlest of gods under your feet," said Caleb.

"Thank you, Caleb. Thank you for everything," said Therion.

Caleb gave Therion a hug then turned to walk off when the Timeless One spoke to him. Caleb turned around and said, "The Timeless One has changed your name. You will no longer be known as Therion, but rather you shall be called Abda for you are new, a worshipper of the Timeless One!"

Caleb left the city and walked back the way he came. As soon as he was out of sight, the Timeless One sent him back to High Rock. Caleb opened his eyes – he was back in the Temple at High Rock. Then Caleb heard the Timeless One say, "Job well done, Caleb."

Eli Zur ran up to Caleb and said "Caleb, what happened? I walked in and saw you heart linking then you were gone. You vanished. As I started over here to see what happened, you appeared out of nowhere. You were just all of a sudden here. You were gone about ten seconds!"

"Calm down, Eli'Zur. Calm down," said Caleb as he put his arm around him. "Let me tell you about my adventure."

They began walking out of the temple. "I wish you could have been there," said Caleb. "The Timeless One took me to heaven and I met the Son............"

To be continued . . .

7

RHYME, RIDDLES AND REASON

*"A wise man will hear and increase learning.
And a man of understanding will attain wise counsel.
To understand a proverb and an enigma.
The words of the wise and their riddles."*

(Proverbs 1: 5, 6 NKJ)

Caleb was in the spirit on the Day of Praise when the Timeless One allowed the man of deception to come to him. He will question him concerning his faith in the Timeless One.

No longer did Caleb stand in his chamber, but now he stood in an unfamiliar place, a place very cold and very quiet. Darkness surrounded him. There were no trees, no grass, and no animals. Stalagmites of all shapes and sizes were everywhere hanging in mid-air. The sky was dark green and, on the horizon, it looked as though there was a great fire. The ground itself was volcanic rock, pure black.

Then from behind a large boulder came the man of deception. He was dressed in a black tuxedo and top hat holding a black cane with a gold handle. He had long black hair, smoking a big cigar and wearing small round black sunglasses. He walked over to Caleb, took the cigar out of his mouth, whipped his head to one side and blew smoke away from him and said, "Look who's here. Could it be? Is it you? Is it me? Look who's here. Now I see. It is you. It is me."

Walking around Caleb he spoke again saying, "High Priest, so brave. High loser, high slave!"

Caleb remained still and did not move. He was not impressed with the man of deception. Caleb was thinking to himself, "Why did the Timeless One bring me here?"

The man of deception took his cane and twirled it like a baton, then slammed it on the ground and said arrogantly, "You are not from here, but I know your name. Can you say the same?"

Caleb crossed his arms and responded in a disgusted voice, "Man of deception, I know your name. If you want, I can play your game."

Then the man of deception walked closer to Caleb, pulled his sunglasses down to the end of his nose, looked over the top of them and said, "Very good high priest, very good indeed. But I am the greatest, soon you will see."

Caleb looked around and found a large rock and sat down. He clasped his hands together and leaned forward on his legs and said, "Tell me man of deception, now tell me true. Why have you rejected the Son and abandoned the Truth?"

The man of deception replied saying, "This is not why you came. This is not why you are here. Now open your eyes, now open your ears."

He took his cane and twirled it around again and did a quick soft shoe, then put both hands on top of his cane and said to Caleb, "Ok High Priest.

Now answer me this and answer me quick. When the rhythm stops, time neither moves forward nor backward. And the one is now two. The one is still but the other is quick to move. Do you have a clue?"

Caleb leaned back on the rock and took a deep breath, let it out slowly and said, "This is your best, man of deception? Life has ceased, death is the reaction."

The man of deception put his cane under his arm, clapped his hands, then took the cigar out of his mouth and said, "Oh good, oh good. What a response. Oh my, oh my, but there's still time."

Caleb stood to his feet and rubbed his hands together and said, "Listen hard. It's my turn. Listen well. And try to learn."

Caleb bent down, picked up a rock, and began rolling it around in his hand. He stared at it for a few seconds. Still looking at the rock he said, "The master extends his arm and grasps the little fool. He moves the little fool, from black to red then back again, at his will for a thrill. In the end, when he will kill."

Looking up at the man of deception he said, "Tell me if you dare, tell me if you rule, who is the master, who is the fool."

The man of deception took his hat off, rolled it down his arm and caught it in his hand. Then he brought it up to his face and looked over the brim at Caleb for a second then put the hat on top of his cane. Again, he took the cigar out of his mouth, blew three rings of smoke in the air then said, "Oh, this is a good one priest, the meaning you hold. Reveal your message, your answer must be told."

Caleb took the rock he still held in his hand and tossed it to the ground. He then walked over and took the cane from the man of deception and quarried, "May I?" He then took the hat and tossed it to the man. Caleb took the cane and twirled it like the man of deception, only better.

He stood the cane on end and rested both hands on the handle and said, "The master is the evilest of creatures that controls the fool at will. The fool is the man of deception who in the end, he will kill."

The man of deception became angry. He threw his cigar to the ground and bellowed, "Lies! Lies! You are full of lies! Truth is not in you! You kill life!"

Then he started to walk away, then stopped and turned around and saying, "A fool I am not! A king I am. A master of rhymes the prince of the damned!"

The man of deception threw his arms up and out spread and asked arrogantly, "When is the creation the creator, and the potter, the clay?"

Caleb stood still and said nothing. He stood there staring at the man of deception. Then he tossed the cane back at the man and still said nothing. The man of deception started pacing back and forth. Then he stopped and looked at Caleb with an evil grin and said, "Hmmmmm, hmmmmmm, a loss for words? Hmmmmm, hummmm. It's going to get worse!"

Then he twirled the cane around his neck, snapped his fingers and a lit a cigar that appeared between his fingers. He took a couple of puffs from it and said, "When the creation creates the creator. And the clay forms the self, He is God."

Caleb became angry. He walked up to the man of deception and got right in his face and said, "Tell me, man of deception, when did you create yourself? And this place, when did you give a worm breath and tell the darkness to flee without a trace? You have crossed the line. For the line was drawn, and you paid no heed; the master of puppets pulled your strings, and you did the deed!"

The man of deception took his cane, whipped it up, and stopped it right between their faces. He leaned to the right side of the cane looking around it and said sarcastically, "Oh brave words priest, mighty and strong. But where do you stand. Is this where you belong?"

Then the man began laughing at Caleb. Then turned and started walking away.

Caleb raised his voice and said, "Man of Deception!"

The man stopped and turned around, "Yes priest?"

Caleb took three steps toward the man and said, "Are you the master? Are you the man? Riddle this, if you can."

The Man of Deception laughed and said, "Oh priest, so naïve. Riddle me, then you will believe."

Caleb put his hands together and brought them up by his face and said, "When all is said and done. You will call your master, the Timeless One."

The Man of Deception took two puffs of his cigar and said, "A riddle for me, a riddle for you. Give me a lie, I'll give you two."

Caleb put his hands behind his back, stood still and said, "A riddle I put before you, a riddle with meaning, a riddle with reason, a riddle with truth."

Then Caleb began walking around the man circling him then said,

"With eyes all about
And no shadow of turning.
From then, to now, to far off.
Penetrating and always burning.
Feeling but not touching
Hearing without sound,
Seeing with visions.
Bringing the sky to the ground."

Caleb stopped in front of the man, reached up, and pulled his sunglasses off. Caleb looked him square in the eyes and said,

"This riddle has reason.
This riddle has rhyme.
Do you have a clue?
Search, that dark mind."

The man of deception grabbed his glasses out of Caleb's hand and in an outrage said,

"You want me to say the name?
To speak of blood and wine?
To speak of your fantasy?
To speak of your crime?"

Then the man took his cane, lifting it up, and pointing with it he said with a stern voice,

"Take flight priest,
Your words are meaningless to the night,
Exit, stage left,
Never to the right."

Then the light from the Timeless One surrounded Caleb. Caleb lifted his hands, palms up as if to heart-link. The stalagmites started falling one by one. The ground began rolling and waving, like water of the ocean, except where Caleb stood. The man of deception tried to run but started sinking. The man began yelling at Caleb saying,

"Cursed is your God,

I will not die,

I . . ."

Caleb still surrounded by the light of the Timeless One interrupted the man as he slowly sank into the ground, calmly he said:

"The eagles have gathered.
The sting is felt,
The Truth is known,
The hand was dealt."

As the man's head was submerged, the ground hardened. All that was left of the man was his hand sticking out of the ground holding his cane and his hat next to it. Caleb walked over and picked up the hat and put it on the cane. Then Caleb said,

"No Fame,
But plenty of pain,
No more games,
To play."

Then the voice of the Timeless One came to Caleb saying, "Well done Caleb. Well done. Again, you have proven your love and trust in Me. Well Done."

Instantly, in a twinkling of an eye he was back in his chamber. Caleb rejoiced and sang a song.

"Most High you are,
Most Ancient and Holy,
Most blessed you are,
Most Loving and Righteous."

When Caleb walked out of his chamber Wah'li'si was standing there. She had come to talk with him about the next Day of Praise Celebration. But when she saw him, she knew, she said to Caleb, "Tell me about your adventure."

To be continued...

8

THE GARDEN

*"The eyes of the Lord are on the righteous.
And His ears are open to their cry.
The face of the Lord is against those who do evil,
To cut off the remembrance of them from the earth."*

Psalm 34:15,16

"Come on Layna. Yes, come on," said Jessica and Petra.

"We're not supposed to leave High Rock alone," said Layna.

"It will only be for a little while," said Petra.

"We won't go far. Come on," said Jessica.

"You've heard Caleb's stories. And what would our parents say?" said Layna.

"We won't go that far, and our parents won't find out," said Jessica.

"Come with us Layna," said Petra. Petra took Layna by the hand, and they went through the gate and away from High Rock.

Jessica, Petra and Layna have been friends since they were very young. Jessica, now sixteen years old, Petra, also sixteen, and Layna, fifteen left the protection of High Rock and ventured out alone. As they walked along the path that leads away from High Rock and towards the bottom of the mountain, they talked and laughed. Before they realized it, they were at the bottom of the mountain and had been gone for hours.

"Wait. Listen!" said Jessica. "Do you hear that?

"Hear what?" said Layna. "Singing! Someone is singing," said Petra.

"It's beautiful," said Jessica.

"Come on!" Jessica and Petra started running toward the sound of the singing.

Layna ran after them shouting, "Stop! Stop! Slow down!" They ran for about half a mile. Then, all of a sudden, they stopped.

"Look at that!" said Jessica.

"Where did that come from?" said Layna.

"I don't know, but it's beautiful," said Petra.

What they saw was a garden. A garden filled with different kinds of flowers and trees. Precious stones littered the ground and a lake that glistened as though it were made of crystal. "The singing is coming from there," said Jessica.

"Let's go see," said Petra.

"No!" shouted Layna. "This isn't right."

"What do you mean?" asked Petra.

"Caleb never told us of a garden out here," said Layna.

"Look, just because Caleb didn't tell us, doesn't mean it was never here," said Jessica.

"Listen to the singing. I must see who is singing. I must see!" said Petra.

Petra and Jessica ran towards the garden. Layna followed. They stopped at the edge of the garden and listened to the singing.

> "Oh, come and see,
> Oh, come and hear.
> The way of the wise,
> A way so dear.
>
> You seek what I have,
> You seek what I give,
> Come and see,
> Come and live."

"Come on!" said Jessica. Petra grabbed Layna's arm and they went into the garden.

As they were stepping into the garden, Layna shouted "NO!" As soon as they were in the garden, Layna grabbed her stomach and fell to her knees.

"Layna, what's wrong?" asked Petra.

"I don't feel too good. We shouldn't be here! said Layna.

"I've got to see who is singing then we'll go," said Jessica.

Layna got up holding her stomach and they went on.

They walked through a patch of willow trees. When they came to the other side of the trees, they saw who was doing the singing.

Three beautiful women all dressed in white silk dresses. They were standing around a circle that was drawn on the ground with one single candle in the center of it.

The women stopped singing, turned and looked at the girls, smiled and walked over to them.

"Hello. Welcome to our garden," said one of the women.

"We heard you singing. We wanted to see who had such beautiful voices," said Jessica.

"Why, thank you. Thank very much. My name is Diana. And these are my two best friends. This is Lilith and this is Rhiannon."

"It was nice to meet you, but we better go now," said Layna as she started to walk away.

"Layna," said Jessica. Layna stopped.

"Please don't leave," said Diana. "Stay just a little while and have some tea,"

"Oh yes, please stay," said Rhiannon. Layna reluctantly agreed to stay for a little while.

"Come," said Diana. "This way."

As they walked further into the garden, Diana got next to Jessica and put her arm around her and asked, "Where do you beautiful ladies come from?"

We live up in High Rock," replied Jessica.

"Do you like it there?" asked Diana.

"Yes! We do," replied Layna sternly.

They all stopped walking and turned to Layna. Diana walked over to her smiling. She reached out to touch Layna on the shoulder, but Layna pulled away before she could touch her.

"Fine," said Diana. "We're here!"

"We are where?" asked Layna.

"The magical place! An enchanted place! A place where dreams come alive, and your fantasies are free to fly," said Diana excitedly.

Lilith walked over to the girls giving them each a red rose and said very softly, "Come and see, feel the breeze. Come and be. So mote it be."

Just then, a soft breeze blew through the trees as Jessica and Petra put the roses up to their faces and smelled them. No one noticed that Layna didn't smell hers. What the girls did not know was that they were slowly being deceived, slowly being put under a spell. Rhiannon walked up behind them. She dipped her finger into a little bowl that had some type of oil in it then held her finger over each of their hearts letting a drop of oil fall on each. As she did this she said, "The perfume of the spirit, the perfume of the he. Blessed are you. Blessed be. So mote it be," Dianna and Lilith echoed "so mote it be."

At this point, Jessica and Petra were in a hypnotic state and Layna was angry, nervous and scared. Dianna walked over by two dogwood trees. They had been trimmed and tied together at the top making an archway. She said in a hypnotic tone, "Follow me to magic. Follow me to wonder. Follow me to wisdom. Follow me to power."

Then she turned and walked through the arch. Jessica followed then Rhiannon, then Petra and then Lilith.

Layna shouted, "Noooooo!" and went through after them. Once she passed under the trees it was like being in another world.

She immediately fell to her knees holding her stomach in pain as before. There was an evil presence here and she knew that they should not be there.

Layna stood and looked around. The ground was pure black and shined like glass. They were in a big open area with trees along the border which no longer had beautiful leaves. In the center of this area, on the ground was a big blood red circle with a five-pointed star in the middle of it with each point touching the circle. At each point of the star was a black candle. In the middle of the star was what looked like an altar draped with a red cloth. Hanging above the altar was a black upside down cross. Jessica and Petra were standing around the circle with Dianna and the other two ladies. Dianna was talking, but Layna couldn't understand her for it sounded as though she was far away even though really, she was just a few feet away. Suddenly they all put their hands together in prayer fashion and bowed their heads. The candle flames grew higher and higher. The cloth that covered the altar fell to the ground. Then from the altar Layna could hear hissing and whispering. Layna was so scared she wanted to run but couldn't get her legs to move. She kept her eye glued to the altar. She knew something was going to happen but didn't know what. Then it happened! Emerging from the altar came a horde of hideous looking demons. Some looked like snakes with heads of lions and some looked like cats with spider legs. They came out and began crawling all over the women standing around the circle. Jessica, Petra and the other ladies didn't move a muscle.

One demon that was on Dianna finally stretched his body out until he was face to face with Layna and said to her in a hissing and wicked voice, "Tell Caleb Plague is back!" then laughed.

Layna began crying, "Ha, ha, ha. I said go! Now! Ha, ha, ha," said Plague.

Layna yelled at Jessica and Petra as they stood in a trance. "I'll be back for you! I promise!" Then she ran.

As she ran out of the garden, she could still hear Plague laughing.

"And tell Caleb I brought the Crown Princes of hell with me! Ha, ha, ha! Run little girl! Run hard! Run fast! Huh! Run!" Softly then he said, "Bring Caleb to me. Bring me, that warrior priest. Run."

Layna ran all the way back to High Rock stopping only long enough to catch her breath then continuing. When she went through the gates, she ran up to Christopher and Logan who were there sparring, just inside the gates.

"Help! Help me!" cried Layna as she fell at their feet.

"Help?" Christopher said as he and Logan bent down to Layna, "Layna! What's happened? What's wrong?"

"Jessica and Petra," she cried out of breath." They're in trouble! I must see Caleb."

"Are they hurt?" asked Logan.

"Not yet," replied Layna. "Please, take me to Caleb, please."

"Come on," said Christopher as he helped her up.

Caleb and Wah'li'si were walking in the vineyard when Christopher, Logan and Layna caught up with them.

"Caleb, Caleb!" yelled Logan

"Logan?" said Caleb. "What is it?" he asked.

"Caleb," sobbed Layna. "Jessica and Petra are in trouble!"

"Calm down Layna," said Wah'li'si as she put her arms around Layna. "Now, tell us what is wrong."

"We left High Rock, that is, me, Jessica and Petra. We left the mountain."

She told Caleb and the others the whole story. "One creature told me to tell you, 'Plague is back,'" she said.

"Plague," uttered Caleb disgustedly.

"Plague!?!" said Logan. "I thought you killed him."

Caleb explained, "There is only One who can kill the disciples of the littlest of gods."

"Then what can we do?" asked Christopher.

"Wah'li'si" said Caleb, "would you take Layna home. Then get Eli'Zur and meet me at the Temple Yard?"

"Yes, Caleb. Come Layna," said Wah'li'si. "But I want to go with you! said Layna.

"Go home. Everything will be alright," said Caleb. Wah'li'si left with Layna.

"I want you two to go and get Ovation and Servant and meet us at the bottom of the mountain tomorrow at noon," said Caleb.

"Yes, Caleb. Right away," said Logan.

"We're gone," said Christopher. "Do not forget your Spirit swords," said Caleb. "Journey safe, journey swift." Caleb hugged Logan, then Christopher then said, "go!"

After they left, Caleb heart-linked with the Timeless One. When he had finished, he sang a song of praise to the Lord.

> "Your glory is here,
> Your power is great.
> Your Spirit shines,
> And You are never late.
>
> Blessed be the name of the Lord,
> Blessed is the Lord Most High
> Blessed is the Ancient of Days,
> Blessed are You, oh God."

When Caleb had finished singing, he left for the Temple Yard to meet Wah'li'si and Eli'Zur.

While all this is happening, Jessica and Petra were still in the Magical Place being deceived. Diana promised them great love and great power if they would bow before the one that bears the light of shadows and renounce The Timeless One. Still hypnotized by the scent of the roses Jessica and Petra got down on their knees and said, "Give us power. Give us love."

Rhiannon and Lilith said, "So mote it be." Plague and the crown princes of hell were laughing and waiting on Caleb.

When Caleb got to the Temple Yard Wah'li'si and Eli'Zur were already there waiting for him. Caleb greeted Eli'Zur with a hug then Eli'Zur said, "What are we going to do?"

Caleb answered saying, "Fast and wait on the Lord. We will know tomorrow at noon."

"Plague will not see another midnight," said Eli'Zur.

Wah'li'si then prayed a prayer of protection over Jessica and Petra. All three lifted their hands as she prayed:

"Mighty God,
Ruler of the Universe and beyond.
Strong in battle, Power with no end.
With the hands that hold the lightening,
...Hold the weak.
With the arms that threw the stars in space,
...Hold the weak.
With the breast that holds the breath of life,
...Hold the weak. Selah.
Amen."

After a moment of silence, Caleb said, "we'll meet back here at dawn. Then go and meet the others at the bottom of the mountain. Rest peaceful." Then they departed and went to their own homes.

When morning came, they met at the Temple Yard. Caleb said a short prayer before they left.

> "Oh, Timeless One,
> Where we go, you have already been.
> You go before us and clear a path.
> We walk in your way.
> Victory is the only end."

When Caleb was finished praying, he looked at Wah'li'si and Eli'Zur with a big smile and a glow about him. Wah'li'si walked over to him and put her hands on his cheeks and looked in his eyes and said, "Caleb, The Timeless One burns in your eyes. Your eyes are aflame."

Caleb reached up and touched Wah'li'si on the hands and with a smile said, "we must go now."

When they got to the bottom of the mountain, Logan, Christopher, Ovation and Servant were already there. They greeted each other with hugs and kisses. "Ovation. Servant, it's good to see you both. It's been a long time. Thank you for coming," said Caleb.

"Yes, it's good to see you too, Caleb," replied Ovation.

"What's going on Caleb?" asked Servant. "Logan and Christopher wouldn't tell us anything, but that you wanted to see us."

"What's wrong Caleb? What has happened?" asked Ovation.

A disciple of the littlest of gods by the name of Plague has come to try to kill me. He has two of our children. I believe he will have them killed shortly," said Caleb.

"Did you say Plague?" asked Ovation.

"Yes. Plague," replied Caleb. Servant and Ovation looked at each other then looked back at Caleb. "Is there something you want to tell me?" asked Caleb.

"It's Plague," said Servant.

"Continue," said Caleb.

Servant said, "This demon has been around for ages. He was a prince on ancient earth before the fall of Lucifer. He followed Lucifer to destruction. He was the one in the Holy Versus, in Acts 19:15 and 16 who attacked the men trying to cast him out. He has possessed thousands of people. Including Mr. Wizard...including me."

"And me," said Ovation.

"This prince of the hell wants you dead," said Servant.

"We're not scared of this bodiless loser!" said Christopher.

"We'll send him back to hell!" said Logan.

"Calm down guys," replied Caleb.

"What are we going to do Caleb?" asked Wah'li'si.

Caleb took a few steps away from the others and turned to face them. He lifted his hands, palms up and said, "Stand still and listen."

A white light came down from heaven and covered them all. Then they could hear an angelic choir singing,

"Holy, Holy, Holy,
The Lord is full of Glory.
Oh, Holy Warrior
You alone are Holy."

Then one by one angels came down from Heaven and stood by each of them. Each angel was holding a golden bowl. Then the voice of the Timeless One echoed in their ears saying:

> "Blessed are you,
> And anointed.
> Blessed are you,
> And sealed.
> Blessed are you
> And filled."

As the Lord spoke the angels each dipped their forefinger into the bowl, they held then pulled it and held their finger over the person they stood by. A sweet oil fell from their finger on to their heart. From head-to-toe Caleb and the others were covered with the sweet anointing oil from God. The Timeless One continued speaking,

> "Go to battle.
> And win, Go to rescue,
> And save,
> Go to conquer,
> And destroy."

When the Lord had finished speaking the light went up, as did the angels. Caleb and the others fell as dead to the ground.

An hour later, they rose up. Their hair was still wet with the anointing oil from the Lord. Wah'li'si and Ovation began singing:

> "The Word is our Song,
> Salvation is our Strength.
> Your Spirit moves in us,
> Like a dancing flame.

"The heavens open up
To show your wonders.
You who made the Universe,
Held me in your arms like a newborn.

"Praise the Lord,
All that breathe,
Praise the Lord
And never cease."

All were in full worship for another hour. All became quiet, then Caleb said, "Let's search and destroy and take back what is ours!" Then they all shouted and left for the garden. They moved like lions chasing their prey. They were at the edge of the garden in minutes.

Standing there, looking before entering, Wah'li'si says, "Beautiful.... but deadly."

"Evil," said Caleb.

A voice from within the garden that said, "Oh, Caleb, my Caleb. Oh, how I've longed to see you."

"Plague," said Caleb.

"I see you brought help again," said Plague.

"As did you, I heard," replied Caleb.

"Show yourself!" yelled Christopher.

Caleb raised his hand towards Christopher in a gesture to "calm down."

"We came for our girls," yelled Caleb.

"They no longer belong to you! They are now part of my coven, ha, ha! They worship me now!" yelled Plague.

"Know this Plague! When the sun sets this day, you won't even be a memory! Your existence will be no more!" shouted Caleb.

Then Plague growled these words:

"Come to me Caleb.

Come and see,

Come now quickly.

Come and bleed!"

Caleb drew his Spirit sword. The others did the same. "The Lord is with us! The Light so shines in our eyes! His Fire burns in our hearts! Every evil thing will bleed the pain of death! Then will be no more! The Lord has given us victory this day! Let us go forth and take back our treasure!" yelled Caleb. Then they all shouted a victory shout and raised their spirit swords in the air.

They entered The Garden and were quickly met by the three witches. "You know what they are," said Logan to Christopher.

Caleb was about to speak to Diana, but she just walked past him like he wasn't there. She stopped in front of Wah'li'si. She spoke to her in two voices at the same time, saying two different things. One was "Who are you?" and the other, "What are you doing here?" Then, she quickly turned to Caleb and said while pointing at him with her finger, "I curse you with an everlasting curse! Death you will taste! Death you will wear! So, mote it be!"

Lilith and Rhiannon repeated, "So mote it be!"

A smoke came up from the ground around them. When it had cleared, Diana and the other witches were gone.

"Cowards!" said Christopher.

"Let's go!" said Caleb. A few minutes into the walk Plague spoke again. "You know, Caleb. I think I need a sacrifice. Yes.

That would please this god very much. Ha! Ha! Ha! Very, very much indeed!" Christopher was about to say something when Eli'Zur put his hand on his shoulder. Christopher looked at him and Eli'Zur just shook his head "no." So Christopher remained silent.

They walked just a little further when they heard women singing. "They try to cast spells with song and dance," said Wah'li'si.

"They conjure in vain," said Logan. When they came to the entrance of the Magical Place, they found standing there in their path a pillar of blue flames. Caleb didn't stop walking, but passed right through the flames without being burned. The others followed and were not harmed. Once through the flames and the arch made at dogwood trees, they were in the Magical Place. The ground was black as coal and as smooth as glass. It was just as Layna had described it; the blood red circle and pentagram on the ground, the altar in the middle of it all.

Caleb noticed someone was lying on the altar. As they moved closer to the altar, Christopher said, "It's Petra!" Her wrists were tied together above her head and her feet were tied together. Christopher started to run toward her. When he got to the edge of the circle, a voice came from the blackness. The voice of Plague saying, "That's far enough." Then from the other side of the circle out of the blackness came Jessica and the three witches. Jessica was still in a hypnotic state and did not recognize Caleb and the others. They stood around Petra in a circle. Then Diana chanted an evocation. Then out of the ground with fire and smoke came Plague and his crown princes of hell. They arrived with screeching, hissing, growls, moaning's and a stench that made one sick to their stomach. The demons ran about the circle in a lunatic manner until they leaped on the witches without them knowing it. They held on to them, picking at their flesh, and still the witches were not aware of it.

Plague moved to the edge of the circle and stood in front of Caleb and growled, "Oh Caleb, my Caleb. So good of you to come!

Do you like my new body?" Plague now had the body of a man wearing a long white robe with a wide red belt, carrying a staff made of gold. Then Plague looked around Caleb and said, "Now who do we have here?" If it's not my two best homes – Servant and Lamentation."

"It's Ovation now! And we now serve the Timeless One!" said Ovation. "We now know true power!" said Servant. "Your incantations, evocation, and mantras from hell are meaningless and empty words that fall to the ground and is no match for the True Power that is about to come upon you!"

"Servant, Servant, Servant. Calm down," mocked Plague as he spun around and started walking towards the altar.

As he kept walking, he never turned back around but said, "Come and witness my perfect, bloody sacrifice in honor of me." At that point, Jessica picked up a knife and held it above her head, ready to plunge it into Petra who lay before here on the altar.

Caleb yelled, "Noooooo!!!" They all rushed towards the altar. The witches began throwing blue fire balls at Caleb and the others.

As Caleb moved towards Plague, he and the others raised their left arm across their bodies as shields of crystal formed in their hands. The fire balls were bouncing off the shields. The demons kept yelling at the witches saying, "More! More! Throw more! Kill! Kill! Kill! More! More!"

Caleb stopped and stared at Jessica although she hadn't moved, he could see tears streaming down her face. Then Plague began dancing wildly in a circle. Slamming his staff up and down on the ground and chanting in an evil growl chanting, "Kill the wicked of the Light! Kill the wicked of God! Kill the servants of the Timeless One! Kill and never stop!" He kept repeating that over and over as he danced.

Eli'Zur, Logan and Christopher ran around the outside of the circle one way while Wah'li'si ran the other way.

Wah'li'si stopped behind Jessica and the others stopped behind the witches. Ovation and Servant stayed in the circle drawing the fire and praying. Plague stopped dancing and jumping up on the altar and held his staff above his head and shouted, "I will have my sacrifice!"

Then Caleb put his shield down and took two steps toward the altar and Plague, then motioned Eli'Zur and Wah'li'si to proceed by saying, "Plague!" he yelled. "Hell awaits!"

At that, Wah'li'si grabbed Jessica and pulled her out of the circle. Jessica fainted outside the circle. At the same time Eli'Zur, Logan, and Christopher came from behind the witches and grabbed the demons by the throat and took their spirit swords and sliced them in half. With a screech, the demons two halves fell to the ground and melted away. Next, they grabbed the witches and dragged them out of the circle. When they got out of the circle, the witches fainted. Then Caleb yelled at Plague saying, "You stand alone Plague!"

"Say goodbye to the little girl!" said Plague.

"Look to the sky Plague...." said Caleb. "Judgement has come! The beginning of your end is now!"

Plague mumbled, "hmmmmm," and looked up. Just then a shaft of light shot down on him. Then two angels flew down on him like eagles attacking their prey. One grabbed him by the arms and the other bound him in chains. They quickly dragged him down to hell.

Caleb ran over, untied Petra and picked her up and carried her out of the circle. The witches and the girls remained unconscious until they were taken out of the garden. Caleb and the others laid them down under a shade tree. When they came around, they had no remembrance of what had happened, or that they had served Plague. None looked back as the garden disappeared.

Caleb then said, "Let us give thanks for a great victory." Then all but the witches raised their hands as Caleb spoke to the Timeless One:

> "We give thanks to You.
> Oh, Timeless One,
> You have shown us mercy.
> And much Love.
> We give you praise.
> And worship only You.
> You are the Victor.
> Once again. King of Glory.
> Amen."

When the hands came down Diana spoke and said, "Who is this king of Glory? Who is this you speak of?" Wah'li'si walked over to her and said, "Let me tell you."

> "He is the Creator of the universe.
> He is the Lover of my soul,
> He fills me with His Spirit.
> He cleans me with his blood.
> He calls to the lonely.
> He calls to the lost.
> He says I love you.
> I love you at all cost."

Diana, Lilith and Rhiannon all said they wanted to know the Timeless One, so Wah'li'si and Caleb showed them the way to freedom and love and introduced them to the King of Glory. Then they all celebrated in song and dance, in clapping and shouting. Ovation lead in a song:

"Add another seat to the table,
Another mansion in being built.
Another crown is being made,
Add one more name to the Book.

(Chorus)
Glory, glory, glory
Glory to the Lamb,
Holy, holy, holy.
Holy is the Lamb.

Welcome to the Family of God
Your sins are washed away.
Welcome to the Family of God.
Your lives will never be the same."

(Repeat chorus)

When they had finished, they went back to High Rock. Diana, Lilith and Rhiannon were invited to live at High Rock for they had nowhere else to go. They accepted.

When they arrived at High Rock, Layna met them at the gate and hugged Jessica and Petra. Everyone gathered at the Temple yard where Caleb told the *Story of the Garden.*

To be continued . . .

9
DREAMS

"And it shall come to pass afterward,
That I will pour out My Spirit on all flesh;
Your sons and your daughters shall prophesy,
Your old men shall dream dreams,
Your young men shall see visions."

Joel 2:28 NKJ

Christopher woke with a shout and in a cold sweat. His heart was pounding, and he was gasping for air. He was terrified of the images he saw in his dream. Holding his head in his hands, he fell back into bed. He stayed there wide awake until dawn, too scared to go back to sleep.

When morning came, Christopher went to see Caleb to tell him of his dream. When he reached the Temple, Eli'Zur was outside feeding Caleb's wolves.

"Eli'Zur" said Christopher.

"Oh, Christopher, what do you need?" asked Eli'Zur.

"I need to talk to Caleb. Is he here?" replied Christopher.

"No," answered Eli'Zur. "He and Wah'li'si are at the amphitheater. They're having band practice."

"Thanks," said Christopher as he ran off towards the theatre.

Christopher got to the amphitheater as they were packing up their instruments. As he approached Caleb, he called out to him "Caleb, Caleb!"

"Christopher," said Caleb with a smile.

"Caleb, I need to talk to you," said Christopher out of breath from running.

"Alright," replied Caleb. "Let's go sit down."

They walked about halfway down the aisle and found some seats.

"What's wrong Christopher?" asked Caleb.

"I had a dream last night," said Christopher as he buried his face in his hand and rested his elbows on his knees. Caleb leaned forward and put his hands on Christopher's back and said, "Tell me about it."

"Alright, I'll try," said Christopher with a sigh.

"I was standing in the middle of a valley. I have never been there before. There were no trees, and the sky was blood red. All around me, everywhere there laid bodies, bodies of dead people – men and women all dead, but no children. There were no children.

"How did they die?" asked Caleb.

"They all had the same wounds" replied Christopher. "They all had these deep cuts across their foreheads, deep gashes in their wrists and holes in their feet. And something else, they were all wet from head to toe. But there was no water in sight and the ground was dry. Then as I fell to my knees and started to cry, a man of ancient times walked up to me and said, 'son, why do you cry?' Then he reached down and helped me to my feet. I asked him what happened to the people and where the children were.

"He answered me saying 'the children are complete.' Then he reached his hand out and stuck it in my chest and pulled out my heart! He held it in front of my face! It was glowing bright! Then he said, 'a perfect heart.' Then with his other hand he pointed to the mass of dead people and said to me, 'they have become like you.' Then, I woke up! What does it mean Caleb? What does it mean?"

Caleb stood and was about to speak when Logan appeared and said, "Caleb, sorry to interrupt, but I had a dream last night and it bothered me very bad." Logan looked over at Christopher and said, "And you were in it man."

"Tell us about it. I had a dream last night too," said Christopher. Caleb put his feet in his seat and sat on the back of his chair. Logan started pacing then began telling about his dream.

"I was standing on top of a high mountain. There was a valley on each side of the mountain. I saw Christopher talking to an old man. They were standing in the middle of the valley surrounded by dead bodies. Bodies were everywhere, but you know, there were no children."

"Dude" said Christopher. "You just described my dream man."

"Continue Logan," said Caleb. "What else happened?"

"Well," said Logan still pacing. "When I looked to the other side of the mountain, I saw a great multitude of people. They were alive but they were in much pain. I saw no wounds, but they all cried out in pain. Again, there were no children. None! Then from the sky I saw mighty angels come down and moved among the people. There were hundreds of them wearing white robes and gold sashes. They carried these black bags that hung at their sides. The people acted like they didn't see them."

"Then, suddenly from behind me, I heard a voice. It sounded like thunder!"

"What did the voice say?" asked Christopher excitedly.

"It said," replied Logan. "'They are not like you. They wished to remain, now, for their reward!' When the voice stopped, the angels stuck their right hand into the black bags they carried and pulled out a handful of red and black, live worms and started dropping them on the heads of the people. As they did this, the people screamed in pain even louder and began to grind their teeth. When I turned to see the voice, no one was there. I fell to my knees and began to cry for the people. And then I woke up. Caleb, what does this mean? How did I see Christopher in his dream? What's going on?"

Just then, Caleb looked up and standing beside him listening to what was being said was James, an artist and songwriter. "Caleb," he said. "I too had a dream." He looked at Christopher and Logan then said, "And you guys were in it."

Christopher jumped up, grabbed James and had him sit in his seat and said, "Tell us man." Caleb never said a word. He just motioned with his hand for James to begin.

"In my dream, I was standing on the side of a mountain. On the side of the mountain behind me was a cave opening. It was too dark to see inside it. When I looked down, I noticed my feet weren't on the mountain, but they were on what looked like transparent gold. A thin layer of gold that stretched across the valley that was before me. Then my body felt like it was burning up on the inside. I reached up and opened my shirt. When I did, my chest opened, and fire came out and stood before me like a pillar. Then a hand came from the pillar and touched my chest. When it did, my skin closed. The pillar of fire moved out over the valley and hovered over the center. As I stood watching a voice came from the fire saying 'Come.' So, I went to where the fire was walking on the thin layer of gold that stretched across the valley. When I reached the fire, the voice came to me again saying,

'With your eyes wide open, look and see!' I looked down through the gold beneath my feet and I saw Christopher and Logan on their knees crying.

They were all alone in the middle of this valley crying. Without looking up, I asked the voice from the fire why they were crying. The voice said, 'One cries for those who have become. And one cries for those who will never be. And both cry for those they haven't seen. Turn and look from where you came.'

"When I turned around to look at the mountain, the cave that was there opened wide and a bright light shown inside. Then out of nowhere appeared seven mighty angels with great swords standing in front of the opening of the cave. Then the voice spoke again saying, 'Go and see what they haven't seen.' So, I walked over to the cave and looked past the angels into the cave."

"What was inside the cave, James?" asked Logan.

"Thousands of children" answered James.

"Children, in a cave?" asked Christopher.

"Inside the cave," continued James "was another valley with trees and green grass. There was even a lake. The children were playing and having fun. When I looked back at the pillar of fire, I was back in my bed. Caleb, can you tell me the meaning?"

Caleb stood and looked to the sky. He said nothing as he lifted his hands, palms up above his head. Christopher, Logan, and James bowed their heads and remained silent. "Thank you," said Caleb. Christopher, Logan and James looked up and saw Caleb smile and bring his hands down, keeping his palms up. He then brushed his hands in front of his face, breathing in as if smelling something wonderful. "The Timeless-One has revealed the meaning of the dreams to me," said Caleb.

Caleb sat on the aisle floor between the seats and began to explain, "This was a special gift the Lord gave you guys. These were more than dreams and visions. These were spirit journeys."

"No way," said Christopher in disbelief.

"Yes" continued Caleb. "You were all in the Spirit world, in God's realm. The Timeless-One was showing you the spiritual side of the physical.

"Christopher, you were in a valley of dead bodies with wounds on their foreheads, wrists and feet. And they were wet from head to toe. The Lord appeared to you as an ancient one. The people are those who have turned to worship the Timeless-One and their spirits are dead to the world. They carry the marks of Christ. The marks on the forehead are made by thorns. The marks on the wrists and feet are made by the nails. For their spirit was crucified with Christ. They are wet because they have been baptized. 'They have become like you.'

"Logan, you saw Christopher because you were in the Spirit world at the same time. You saw people without wounds walking around. But they were in pain. The Timeless-One came to you as a voice. Now, the voice said, 'They are not like you. They wish to remain." Those people are they that did not turn from their evil ways. They do not worship our Lord. They do not wear the marks of Christ. Their spirit is tormented by the worms of hell. These worms will torment them even when their bodies die.

"And James, in the Spirit world, you saw Logan and Christopher crying over the people, and the children they didn't see, but you saw them. The Lord appeared to you as a pillar of fire and revealed to you that the children are protected by guardian angels and sheltered by the Mighty Rock of Offense. Lastly, the fire represents the power of the Holy Spirit.

"Take delight gentlemen, in these Spirit journeys. For the Lord has seen in each of you, greatness in faith, love, and wisdom. You each have the heart of a champion, and the desire of a warrior.

Remain in the Lord, and His power. You are not a flame but a great fire. The Spirit journeys have just begun for you. You guys are going to have many, many more travels in the Spirit. Many more...."

When Caleb was through, they all jumped to their feet and shouted to the Lord and praised His Holy name. They worshipped the Timeless-One for over an hour. When they were finished, they talked among themselves wondering what their next journey would be like.

To be continued . . .

10

LIQUID CHRIST

"For you will light my lamp;
The Lord my God will enlighten my darkness."

Psalms 18:28

"And that is why the Timeless-One sent His only Son, the Word to earth to die for our sins," said Wah'li'si to the children around her. They sat under a very large willow tree by the flowing stream.

"Wah'li'si," said a little girl, "You're very pretty."

Wah'li'si embarrassed, said "Thank you Faith."

"You have a pretty name too. What does it mean?" asked another little girl.

"Well thank you again," said Wah'li'si. "It's an ancient word from an ancient race of people that I am proud to be one of. The people and the language is Cherokee. The meaning is, 'sweet as a honey dew'."

The children said, "That's pretty."

Caleb sitting beside her reached around her and tugged on each of her cheeks and said, "And she is sweet as a honey dew." The children started laughing. Wah'li'si playfully hit Caleb on the shoulder and laughed, "You!" Just then they heard a high pitch humming coming from the sky. They looked up and saw six round balls of green fire. They moved across the sky very quickly and disappeared. "The littlest of god," said Caleb. "Alright children," said Wah'li'si, "we must go now. Why don't you go to the park and play?"

"Ok. Ok," said the children as they ran off to play. Caleb looked at Wah'li'si and said, "Let's head back to the Temple.

When they arrived at the Temple yard, there standing in the middle of the yard was the Timeless-One in the form of a pillar of white fire. As soon as Caleb and Wah'li'si saw this, they fell to their knees and put their faces to the ground. The Lord spoke to Caleb saying "The heavens rejoice over your deeds, and the way you serve your God and your people. They say, 'There's a man of God, a man of action and a man of love.' Heaven knows we can count on you and the people of High Rock."

Caleb and Wah'li'si remained kneeling and did not move. Wah'li'si did not hear the Timeless-One speak.

"Caleb, my beloved servant," continued the Lord, "The littlest of gods has sent his disciples of deception to the Village of Fences." The white pillar of fire turned dark scarlet then the Timeless-One spoke again, "Caleb, High Priest stand and receive beautiful wisdom. She will burn as the Holy Spirit burns within you." Caleb stood and lifted his hands to the sky, palms up. Just then, the pillar of scarlet fire rose in the air and moved to hover over Caleb. The Lord spoke with a loud voice saying, "Receive!" the fire fell on Caleb then quickly shot up to Heaven.

Caleb remained there with his hands still lifted high. His hair was dripping wet with oil. Wah'li'si slowly rose to her feet. She saw the pillar of fire was gone and looked over at Caleb. She knew he had been with God.

Caleb brought his hands down. He looked at Wah'li'si and said, "We must go to the Village of Fences."

"Alright," replied Wah'li'si.

Caleb lifted his hands once again and said a prayer:

"Oh Timeless-One,
With your sweet anointing oil
You bathe me.
With Your sweet Holy Spirit
You baptize me.

"Wisdom is so precious,
She is so lovely.
She is so gentle.
And so full of power.

"Oh Lord full of glory
You have illuminated my soul.
And enlightened my mind.
You have filled my heart with love.
And my eyes with fire.

"Blessed be the name of the Lord.
Blessed is the Lord Most High.
Blessed is the Ancient of Days.
Blessed are you oh, God."

Caleb brought his hands down. Wah'li'si said, "Caleb, you have been blessed."

After this, people began gathering in the Temple yard around Caleb asking about the green balls of fire that passed across the sky.

Caleb spoke to the people calmly but with assurance and authority saying, "The green fire balls you saw are agents of the littlest of gods. You are not in any danger, but the Village of Fences is." At that moment six more green fire balls went over head following the same path as the others. Caleb called out, "Eli'Zur, Christopher, Logan, and Rapha, I need to speak to you. The rest please go home and heart-link with the Timeless-One for the safety of the people of the Village of Fences."

The people went home and the ones he named stayed behind as did Wah'li'si. They all gathered on the steps of the Temple. "Eli'Zur, I need you stay at High Rock and be with the people," said Caleb.

"As you wish," replied Eli'Zur.

"The rest of us are going to the Village of Fences," said Caleb. "Rapha,"

"Yes?" answered Rapha.

"I would like for you to join us," said Caleb. "Your knowledge of the heavens and your understanding of the universe may be needed."

"I would be honored to be part of your holy regime," replied Rapha.

Caleb smiled and said, "Good."

Logan and Christopher slapped him on the back and said, "Alright!"

"Alright then," said Caleb. "We will meet back here tomorrow morning one half hour before sunrise, rest easy." Then they all went their separate ways.

Wah'li'si and Caleb faced each other, held hands and looked at each other in silence for about a minute. Then Wah'li'si said, "Rest easy Caleb."

"Rest easy," replied Caleb. Wah'li'si turned and went home.

Caleb went into the Temple and heart-linked with the Timeless-One. When he was finished, he sang to the Lord:

> "Lord of heaven and earth.
> God of the universe and beyond,
> Ruler of the galaxies
> Lord of host You are.
>
> "Lord of heaven and earth.
> God of the universe and beyond,
> Ruler of the galaxies
> Lord of host You are."

When Caleb was finished praising the Lord, he went to his room and lay down on his bed to asleep. Before he fell to sleep wondered, "Why has the Timeless- One chosen me? I am not worthy of His grace and of His love. I am just a man; I am just dust that the wind will scatter. I . . ..." The Timeless-One interrupted him and whispered, "Hush, now sleep." Caleb immediately fell to sleep.

When all were asleep, they, the holy regime, all had the same dream. They all stood in the Temple yard in a circle with their hands held high, palms up. The Word then came down from on high and stood in the middle of them and spoke saying, "Go, and remove the mask. Go and open the eyes. Go with hearts of fire. Go and trample the fences and the evil under feet. Go! You shall not walk! For I will take you! It is time!" Then they all woke up at the same time. It was morning.

When they all arrived back at the Temple yard, no one said a word because in the middle of the yard was a figure made of white light. They all stood staring at it. Then a voice came from it saying, "Come."

Then Caleb and the others went and stood around the figure of light.

"Oh Lord!" said Christopher as he fell to his knees. The others went to their knees as well. A swirling wind started blowing as they all started worshipping saying, "Holy, Holy, Holy are you God. Holy, Holy, Holy."

Then a voice came from the figure of light once again saying, "I am the Light of the World! Go and tell the lost!"

In an instant, they were just one hundred feet from the Village of Fences, still kneeling in a circle. Then the Light shot up into heaven. The voice came to them again saying, "It is their time."

Wah'li'si broke out in a song of praise:

> "Holy is the Lord.
> And worthy to be praised.
> Holy is the Lord,
> His majesty Reigns.
>
> He's shown us a mystery.
> He's shown us truth.
> He's given us wisdom.
> And made our hearts brand new.
>
> Oh, the mystery of Your love,
> The hidden treasures of Your heart.
> One ounce of Your living water,
> Satisfies a thousand galaxies.
> Selah,
> Amen!
> Everyone, Amen."

Caleb then said, "The windows of heaven have been opened. Blessing has been poured out on us."

Then everyone said, "Amen."

"Let's go," said Caleb. Then they headed for the village. When they entered the village gate, they were met by a man and woman from the village.

"Welcome strangers," greeted the woman. Their skin had a glittering metallic look to it and their eyes were black." Have you come to see the Enlightened Elect and drink of the Liquid Christ?" asked the man.

"Liquid Christ?" said Christopher in disbelief.

"We have come, to see the Enlightened Elect," said Caleb.

"Well, then follow us. We'll take you to them," said the woman.

As they walked through the village, Wah'li'si whispered to Caleb saying, "Have you noticed all the people have the same empty smile on their face."

"Yes, and everyone's skin is metallic looking," replied Caleb.

When they reached the center of town, they were led into a large open area. Surrounding the area were the twelve green fire balls. Each ball was about twelve feet in diameter. As they passed by them, Rapha reached out to touch one, because the fire balls weren't putting out any heat. As he came in contact with the fire, his hand passed through the ball like it wasn't there, but the fire was ice cold. In the center of this area was what looked like a ceremonial site. At the northern part of this area was a very tall metallic cross. To the southern point of the area standing on end was an inverted pentagram made out of the same material with three roses woven through it. To the east was a statute of Buddha with an ankh behind him. Then to the west was an inverted triangle encircled by a snake swallowing its tail.

To the north where the cross was, Caleb noticed what looked like an altar with a silver chalice on it. Six thrones lined each side of the altar. Stopping in the center of the area the man said, "Wait here." Then the man and woman left.

Then, from out of nowhere two hands emerged in the air in front of the cross, behind the altar. As if removing bricks from a wall, they were taking pieces of space and making a black hole. As the hole in space and time was being made, evil and wicked sounds came from within it such as an erratic heartbeat, hissings and chirping. A smoke and a very strong stench emanated from within it. "I know that stench," said Logan to Caleb.

"So do I," replied Caleb.

When the hands were through making the hole, they disappeared. Then, one by one, beings came walking out from within the black hole. They were bald with silver skin and pure black eyes. They wore sleeveless black robes and no shoes. As they came through, they each went and stood in front of a throne. Once they were all through and standing in front of the thrones, they sat down at the same time. They black hole remained.

Then one of the beings stood and spoke saying, "You are not from here. Come and drink the Liquid Christ and you will be like us -- enlightened and all knowing – at peace and at one with the universe."

Caleb took a few steps forward and said, "We did not come here to become like you, but to expose and destroy you and bring the Truth and the Light of the Word to the people of this village."

"But we are truth, and we are light. We are part of the All and the All is part of us," said one of the beings.

Then another being stood and said, "The All has made many worlds and there are many worlds in the All. Our world was the first to be made by the All. Before time was measured, we are."

Still another stood and spoke, "We are Solar Logos the Enlightened Elect from the world Sylphs Eden."

Rapha stepped forward and said, "Where is Sylphs Eden located?"

"Your star charts are not advanced enough to locate our world. It lies three million light years past the edge of your known galaxy."

Rapha looked at Caleb and asked, "May I?" Caleb motioned with his hand to continue.

Then Rapha took two more steps forward and said, "Tell me, how long did it take you to get to our planet?"

"We travel from world to world by thought," said another being. "The All is in us, and we are in the world and the world is in the All. We, the Solar Logos the Enlightened Elect go where we wish by a wish. And you can too. Just drink the Liquid Christ and you will be one of us. Just as this village has been enlightened by the All, so can you." Now being picked up the chalice and held it out in front of him towards Caleb. He invited them, "Drink the Liquid Christ and be saved from this world of false light and false hope. Become enlightened by the All."

"Release these people of your spell and climb back in your hole!" yelled Christopher, "Or, we'll send you back to hell ourselves!"

"Such a primitive world," said the first being. "You still believe in a place called hell."

"Don't you?" asked Logan. "That's where you're from."

"There is no heaven. There is no hell," said another being. "You are the creator of your own world and your own destiny. You can have the mind of the Christ and the power of the Solar Logos with one drink of the Liquid Christ."

The people of the village began gathering outside the area listening to what was going on within the circle of the fire balls.

Caleb walked up to the being holding the silver chalice and carefully took it from his hands. The being said, "Yes, become enlightened. Become one with the Universe."

Caleb turned and faced Wah'li'si and the others and took three steps toward them. Then, he lifted the chalice above his head and shouted, "The charade is over! It is time to unmask the masked!" Holding the chalice with both hands, he brought it down slowly as he said, "Unveil the veiled! Reveal the hidden. Open the eyes that are closed!"

When he had finished saying this, lightening came down from heaven striking the green fire balls. The fire balls disappeared one by one with a puff of smoke and a cracking sound. The people were now able to see what was going on with the strangers and the Enlightened Elect.

Christopher and the others drew their spirit swords and stood ready. Then Caleb said to the people of the village, "Look at the Liquid Christ! Look upon their evil deceptions." Caleb slowly poured out the contents of the chalice. As the liquid started falling from the chalice it quickly turned into demonic winged maggots. As they hit the ground, they swarmed to the black hole. Caleb took the chalice and threw it to the ground. Then, he took his right foot and stomped on it smashing it under his heel. When he did this the demons in the villagers began leaving them, crawling out of their mouths and their eyes flying back through the black hole. The people then fell unconscious.

The Enlightened Elect began changing form. They started growling and moaning. They were hissing and screaming. Their skin was falling off in chunks as if it had died and rotted. Under the skin, the Enlightened Elect showed their true form.

Now standing only three feet tall, with green scaly skin, all twelve had one horn coming from right between the eyes. They ran around and encircled Caleb and the others showing their claws and razor-sharp teeth.

Then one of the elect spoke in a slurring and hissing voice saying, "SOOO Priest now you know!" The other demons were spitting and vomiting at them. "After we kill you," continued the demon, "We will rip the flesh off the villagers and eat them alive!"

"Demon!" said Caleb, "You have not yet understood that you are subject to the Highest of High! The Master of galaxies!" As Caleb spoke the demons went into the frenzy, "The Alpha and the Omega, the Beginning and the End, the I Am!" The demons kept circling Caleb and the others, spitting at them, hurling blasphemies and obscenities, growling and jumping up and down saying, "We're going to kill you, Caleb! And rape Wah'li'si! Yes! I'm going to eat Christopher's eyes!"

Caleb continued, "Almighty God, The Ancient of Days, the King of Glory, Prince of Peace!"

"Silence priest!" screamed one of the demons. "You must stop!" The demons moved faster around them still yelling and growling threatening to kill Caleb and the others.

Caleb continued speaking. Logan and the others held their Spirit Swords out and ready. "Lover of Souls, the Lord of Hosts, Lord God Omnipotent!" Then Caleb said with a very loud voice, "The slayer of demons!" The demons stopped and with a painful scream they leaped on the points of the swords and disintegrated.

"Whoo hoo!" said Christopher. "The Timeless-One never ceases to amaze me. Wow!"

Then Caleb walked toward the people and to the ones with him. "Lift your hands to the Timeless-One." As they did, he said, "Oh Timeless-One renew their hearts, their minds, and their souls." When he had finished speaking, the spirits of the villagers rose out of their bodies. Then fire came down from heaven and landed on the spirits then shot back up to heaven.

The spirits went back into the bodies. Then they stood to their feet praising the Lord in unknown languages and in dancing. This lasted for an hour.

When they had stopped, the leader of the village came to Caleb and thanked him.

Caleb and the others stayed at the village for a week teaching the people the ways of the Timeless-One. When they left, they gave the leader a copy of the Holy Verses. As they walked out of the village, Christopher said, "Another story huh Caleb?"

To be continued . . .

11

THE VISION OF A SATANIC INTERVIEW

"And it shall come to pass afterward
That I will pour out My Spirit on all flesh;
Your sons and your daughters shall prophesy,
Your old men shall dream dreams,
Your young men shall see visions."

Joel 2:28 NKJV

Then the Timeless-One said, "Take what I have shown you in your mind's eye Caleb and tell the people of High Rock. Tell them what you witnessed. Tell them the things you saw and the things you heard. Leave nothing out."

This was the morning of the Day of Praise, and everyone had gathered in the Temple waiting for the morning reading of the Holy Verses. Caleb walked onto the platform and stopped behind the podium. All was quiet. He then walked to the edge of the stage and sat down with his feet hanging down the side and said, "I'm not going to read from the Holy Verses today.

The Lord has given me a vision to share with you. Listen close. This is what I saw, and this is what I heard."

"I was in a theater sitting with the audience facing a large stage. In the center of the stage were two plush chairs. One was empty; the other had a man with the fire in his eyes and strength on his face. This is the host. There was much excitement and anticipation in the auditorium. No one was speaking. You could hear a pin drop.

"Then the host spoke to a man I couldn't see saying, HOST: Is he here?

MAN: Yeah. Are you ready?

HOST: I'm ready.

MAN: Ok. We're on in five, four, three, two, and one.

HOST: Hello. Welcome to this week's show of *Myth, Magic, or Miracle*. I'm your host Elijah David. Our show is a little different this week. We have a guest, an unusual guest. You know him and yet, you don't know him. Well, let's bring him out. From far beyond the river Styx and from roaming to and fro throughout the earth, here he is – the Son of Sin, Satan.

(No applause, stone silence.)

SATAN: Thank you. Thank you. Thank you.

"He came from behind the curtain that hung behind the chairs. He was dressed in a white suit with a black shirt and red tie. He had short black hair, slicked back and a big smile, waving like he was running for office. He walked over to the host and bowed to him and sat down."

HOST: Before we begin, how would you like to be addressed?

SATAN: You may address me as The Illuminator.

HOST: The Illuminator?

SATAN: Yes. For, I am the light bearer. "He said arrogantly." I open men's eyes to the world around them. Even your Holy Verses says that I come as an angel of light. So, I am the Illuminator.

HOST: Now, your former state was Lucifer the Light Bearer but aren't you now, Satan, the enemy of God?

SATAN: This is true. Your God and I are enemies.

HOST: It wasn't always this way though.

SATAN: No, it wasn't. In my beginning I was Archangel Lucifer' the bearer of great light. I walked among the stones of fire that lay before the throne. I oversaw the music in heaven for I am music. I was the fifth living creature. I was full of beauty and power. I myself had followers. I ruled a third of the angels in heaven. They are with me now.

HOST: What was the reason for you leaving heaven?

"Satan leaned forward; his eyes turned pitch black and with a deep growl said,"

SATAN: I was thrown out . . . David!

HOST: Tell us, why you were thrown out of heaven.

"Satan relaxed in his chair and calmed down. Smiling again he said,

SATAN: My beauty. My intelligence. My desire to be God, maybe. I personally blame Jesus. If it wasn't for him, I would be in heaven right now at God's right hand! Jesus was very jealous of me! Very jealous!

HOST: You mentioned you oversaw the music in heaven. Do you still have an interest in music?

SATAN: Ah, David, yes, most definitely. I have my hand in every kind of music there is.

One style of music is to clear your mind of thoughts, including thoughts of your God. Another style is used for, let's say getting drunk, raising hell and committing adultery, the way good ole boys have a good time. And still another style is used to corrupt the youth and destroy their morals. I destroy their minds and bodies! I steal the souls! I get them drunk and rape your girls! I get them high and stoned then crush them with suicide and murder. Some openly worship me. All this using music. This is a perfect medium for a perfect crime. I see you're amazed at my intelligence. One day all people will openly worship me!

"Satan leaned back again in his chair and with an evil grin said,"

I'll tell you something else I'm very much into, is the image screens. People are mesmerized and hypnotized by the image screens. They are so numb to the evil and wicked things I set before their eyes, such as sex outside of marriage, gay love, adultery, abortion, blasphemy and the occult. The youth can't live without the image screen. The anti-God style of living will always be in front of the eyes always being messaged into their minds. When the young are weak, then, my philosophy I will preach, and they love it. Hahahahaha!

HOST: So, your main goal is to corrupt the youth. Am I right?

SATAN: You are correct.

HOST: Why?

SATAN: Simply put, if I can get the youth, then I have the future. If I can change their thoughts about me and change their morals. If I can just keep them occupied on winning the game or getting to the next level, I will destroy them. I will kill them! Oh, I love to kill children! I kill them mentally, physically, and spiritually! Oh, how I love to kill children! I kill, and I will always kill! And one day I will kill that so called God in heaven! I will sit on that throne and all people will worship me!

"The host, Elijah David was bothered by all he heard, but remained calm.

HOST: Now, do you really believe that?

"With a smirk, Satan then lit up a cigar and said:"

SATAN: Watch me. I have many followers; many, many followers. They do whatever I command. They rape for me. They steal for me. And they kill for me. My followers are those who took prayer out of the teaching halls. My followers are those that preach fornication and adultery is natural and not a sin. They also say men are basically smart animals. Some even say I don't exist. That's my favorite. Hahahaha! My followers will bring me into power very shortly – very, very shortly.

HOST: Alright! Let's move on. You have many names you go by. Why?

SATAN: One word: deception! Or you could call it confusion. Maybe, distraction. You see, most people can't openly, knowingly worship me. They have a problem with the name Satan. As you know if a person doesn't worship God, they must worship someone. It's human, your human need to worship. See if you can recognize any of my aliases: Beelzebub, Bail, Kali, Cernunnos, Baphomet, Krishna, Buddha, Pan, Zeus, Earth, Money…..Self. And the list goes on and on and on. The funny thing is, they're all me. If you don't worship the God, you worship me! ME!

HOST: So, your main objective is to turn and keep people away from God. And eventually kill them. Is this correct?

SATAN: That is correct.

HOST: Reason?

SATAN: Very simple really. God is love. I hate God and love! God loves you! I hate you! I hate everybody and everything! Right now, I can't have my true throne! The throne your God sits on! And right now, I can't touch your so-called God, but, but I can hurt Him! Oh yes, I can hurt Him!

"David became very angry."

HOST: What?!?

SATAN: I said, I CAN HURT HIM!!!

HOST: Tell me, how can you hurt the All Powerful Ancient of Days?

SATAN: Every time I turn someone from Him, every time I kill an unborn baby, every time I have a virgin sacrificed or get a teenager stoned and suicidal. I hurt Him. My biggest thrill and His biggest hurt is when I kill children. I LOVE TO KILL CHILDREN! My goal is to kill you and God! Those I haven't killed will worship me! I will sit on my throne above the clouds and reign forever and use you as my footstool.

HOST: Just minute! God created you! Now, how……

"Satan became furious. Horns started growing out of his head and his eyes became black as coal. He started growing fangs and foaming at the mouth. He stood to his feet, faced David, put his hands on the arms of the chair and leaned forward."

SATAN: That is a lie! I am perfect! That Jesus created that story and told all the galaxies. Now, all of heaven and earth believe Him! Now, He's up there and I'm down here but that will soon change! I will kill Jesus! I will take my throne back! I will take Him down! I killed Him once and I'll kill him again! And this time, He will stay dead!

"Satan stood up straight and straightened his tie and suit."

HOST: You can't honestly believe that?

SATAN: Look! I have already corrupted this earth and its people. I have put doubt in the heart of men. Good is now evil, and evil is now good. I have destroyed everything your God has created in one way or another! Even His Son! I crucified Jesus once…. I can do it again! And I will!

HOST: But I have read in the Holy Verses that say when a Christian speaks the name of "Jesus" to you and your demons, you run!

SATAN: Run?!? That is a false statement! Answer me this? Have you ever seen God?

HOST: No, I haven't....

"Satan started pacing back and forth in front of David."

SATAN: So, how do you know He's real?

HOST: Because I......

SATAN: You know the Bible is a myth, a fairytale! A book of lies! You know I'm right!

HOST: Look, you are....

"David now stood to his feet."

SATAN: I am the almighty! I am the true god! I wrote the Bible! Your life and everyone's life is all a game for me! It's like having an ant farm. There is no Jesus! There is no heaven! There is no hell! There is no God! I am the only one out there! I am....

"David stepped in front of Satan and held his out in front of him."

HOST: This interview is over Satan! I rebuke you in the name of Jesus! Go back to your hell, NOW!

"Satan disappeared in a puff of smoke. The audience stood and cheered. As did I"

As soon as Caleb finished everyone in the Temple stood and shouted, whistled and applauded. And everyone was encouraged. Then Wah'li'si lead everyone in praise and worship.

To be continued . . .

12

CORRIDORS

"I will love You, O Lord my strength.
The Lord is my rock and my fortress and my deliverer.
My God, my strength in whom I will trust.
My shield and the horn of my salvation, my stronghold."

Psalm 18:1, 2 (NJKJV)

As Caleb heart-linked with the Timeless-One, the Word came to him and said, "The littlest of Gods wishes to put you and your holy regime to the test. He hates you Caleb, with a "great hate."

"As I do him," replied Caleb.

"Be ready my beloved Caleb," continued the Word. "Be strong and courageous. I will never leave you nor forsake you."

When the Word had finished speaking, He was lifted up. Caleb then stood alone in the Temple. He brought his hands down and with authority in his voice, he said,

"To be tested,

Is to be made strong!

To be attacked,

Is to crush the head of Satan!"

He turned and walked to the back of the Temple to leave, when he walked thru the door and shut it, but instead of being outside in the Temple courtyard, he found himself in a very large red room. Across the room was a very long corridor. On either side were doors. As far as he could see, there were doors. Then he heard a voice saying in a loud echo, "Caleb, High Priest of High Rock, and Servant to the Timeless-One. You have been found guilty of numerous war crimes. You and your foolish followers are charged with murder and torture. You have brutally murdered thousands of my army of dark forces and therefore you shall stand trial for your deeds."

"You attack children and the kill the innocent!" Caleb yelled back.

"Through the Timeless-One we defended the defenseless! If that means throwing your pigs of war into nonexistence, then so be it!"

"That's enough!" shouted the littlest of gods. "Before you is the mystic maze, the corridor of corruption," continued Satan. "Find your way to the end and receive judgment. Along the way you will gain the agony and ecstasy, prizes and pain."

Caleb stood looking down the corridor saying nothing.

"You may continue," said Satan in the loud deep echo. "Your prizes await you and judgment must be carried out."

Caleb stepped into the corridor, as he did a wall formed behind him sealing him in. So, there is no turning back – not that he wanted to.

As Caleb walked down the corridor, every step he took echoed. About halfway down the hall of doors, he could see that it was a dead end. So, he stopped and decided to open one of the doors.

He turned to his right and opened the door. He stepped into the doorway; the room also was all red. In the middle of the room, he saw Logan chained to the floor by the ankles.

"Caleb," yelled Logan.

"Logan!" said Caleb as he ran over to him. Caleb grabbed the chains that bound Logan to the floor and began pulling on them, trying to free his brother.

"It's no use Caleb. It's no use," said Logan.

"Faith, brother, faith. Power and strength come from the Holy Spirit that burns within us!" said Caleb with authority in his voice.

Caleb stood to his feet lifting his hands, palms up and tilted his head back as if to heart-link with the Timeless-One. He stood that way for about ten seconds, and then with his right hand, he pulled a flaming white sword out of thin air. In one motion, he brought it down and struck the chains and shattered them, freeing Logan. Caleb fell to his knees in praise. Logan laid face down in worship saying, "Deliverance is in the name of the Lord! Holy is the God of my Salvation!"

"Amen," said Caleb.

When they stood to their feet, they looked around the empty red room. The door Caleb entered though had vanished and a wall had taken its place. On each of the other walls were doors, then echoing in their ears came the voice of the littlest of gods saying "Choose wisely, choose wrong. The magic is true. The magic is strong."

"What do you think?" asked Logan.

"Let's open a door," said Caleb. Logan walked over to the door on his right and opened it. As he did, a wind gust through the room. On the other side of the door was nothing but blackness and empty space. Suction from the black space began pulling Logan through. Logan was holding on to the door. Caleb ran over and pulled Logan back and slammed the door. Logan, standing bent over with his hands on his knees then looked up at Caleb (the wind had quit blowing) and said, "Wrong door."

Caleb walked over to Logan and put his hand on his back and said, "You think?" He put his arm around him and said, "My turn." Caleb went to the door across the room and opened it. On the other side was another corridor. "Let's try it," he said.

As soon as they walked through the door, it vanished. They turned to look back but didn't see the door they walked through, nor did they see the room they had been in. What they did see was a sea of blood and fire. "Gaze upon your destiny. Look upon your judgment," echoed the littlest of gods. "Come on," said Caleb as he and Logan turned to walk down the corridor.

When they got about halfway down the corridor Caleb felt compelled to stop and open a door. He opened one on one side of the hall and Logan opened one on the other side. Simultaneously they called out "Wah'li'si!" They turned and looked at each other and said "What?"

"Wah'li'si is over here!" said Logan.

"She can't be! She's chained to a post in this room!" replied Caleb.

"What do we do?" asked Logan.

"You go in your room, and I'll go in mine!" said Caleb.

"Let's do it," replied Logan.

Again, as they stepped through the doorways, the doors closed and vanished behind them. Once in, they realized they were standing side by side in the same room. "This is nuts," said Logan.

"Caleb!" yelled "Wah'li'si. She was in the middle of the room chained to a pole made of black metal. She was standing with her back to the pole and her hands chained together, stretched above her head and linked to a metal ring on top of the pole. Caleb and Logan started to run to her. They took a couple of steps when from behind her came two disciples of the littlest of gods each standing about four feet tall having bodies of frogs although they walked upright. Their faces were also that of a frog, but their mouths were full of long razor sharp teeth with foamy saliva stringing from their mouths. Long greasy hair covered their heads. Holding long spears in their hands, one said in a slurring speech, "Try to rescue her and die, Priest!"

Then from above came two white balls of fire which rested in midair in front of Caleb and Logan. Caleb reached out and took a fire ball in his hand. Logan saw what Caleb had done and did the same. The fire did not burn them. Then Caleb yelled at the demons saying, "As the Timeless-One forever lives, you shall forever die!" Caleb and Logan threw the fireballs at the demons, who exploded into a fine dust. Then the chains that held Wah'li'si fell to the ground. Wah'li'si went to Caleb and hugged him saying "What's that gnat up to now, Caleb? Where are we?"

"The worm has put us on trial for war crimes."

"Trial? War crimes?" said Wah'li'si in disbelief. Just then, the floor they stood upon vanished. They fell onto a large slide and slid down, spiraling and twisting. Loud hissing and demonic laughter echoed in their ears. It was totally dark with flashes of lightening. When the ride ended, they fell on the floor in another room where Christopher and Rapha were.

"Nice of you to drop in," said Christopher as he and Rapha went over to help them up. "Anybody want to tell me what's going on?" asked Christopher.

"The littlest of gods," said Logan.

"Of course," replied Christopher.

After realizing where they were, Logan says, "You've got to be kidding!"

"One way out," said Rapha.

They stood on a circular floor of about fifty feet in diameter that seemed to just float in midair for all around them was complete nothing. There was one door, and it was about three hundred feet away from where they stood. There was no floor between them and the door but total blackness. From the blackness came demonic screams saying, "Come down to us Priest! Hell awaits your arrival!"

Then Caleb said, "Gather around and lift up holy hands."

They all came in close together and lifted their hands toward Heaven, then Caleb spoke saying,

> "When morning breaks,
> You greet us with Heaven's kiss.
> At the heart of noonday,
> The shade of Heaven wings.
> When night falls,
> Your songs of love and grace,
> Comforts us."

"'Faith is the substance of things hoped for, the evidence of things not seen,' says the Lord of Glory," said Wah'li'si with authority in her voice.

"For we walk by faith, not by sight, says the Ancient of Days!" shouted Christopher.

"The effective, fervent prayer of a righteous man avails much says the Painter of Sunset," proclaimed Rapha.

"As for our Redeemer the Lord of Hosts is His name!" shouted Logan.

Then Caleb spoke saying, "The Holy Verses declare, 'Stand still and see the salvation of the Lord!'"

Just then, the Word came to them and stood at the edge of the platform where they stood. All fell face down on the floor in worship.

"Arise," said the Word. "Arise and walk."

Caleb and the others stood to their feet and looked upon the Word. The Word stretched out His arms and said, "Come. Walk in love. Walk in power. Walk in the blood."

Caleb walked to the Word. He stretched out his arms as if to hug him then passed right through Him. Once on the other side of Him, Caleb was standing on the air. Being fully filled with the Fire of the Holy Spirit he walked across the black abyss in midair to the door. Once he crossed over, the Word said to the others, "Come." He nodded and smiled to let them know it's alright and said again, "Come." Then one by one they walked through Him and walked on the air to the other side. Once they all got to the other side and went through the door, the Word vanished. Then all went into worship and with one voice they all sang:

> "Holy, Holy, Holy.
> The Lord is full of Glory.
> Holy, Holy, Holy,
> Our Promise, Our Star of the Morning."

Again, the door shut and vanished. Ahead of them was another long corridor. "Priest!" echoed the voice of the littlest of gods." I see the Timeless-One has helped you again. I also see there is someone missing from your little group. To find him is one thing. To save him is another. Ha, ha, ha!"

"Eli'Zur!" shouted Christopher. "We've got to find him!"

"Calm down Christopher. We'll find him," said Caleb. "Let's go."

As they walked down the corridor, Christopher, Rapha, and Logan opened every door but behind every each was a solid wall. When they finally reached the end of the hall it dead ended. The hall neither went to the right or the left. But there was one door, and it was cracked open. Caleb walked over to it and slowly pushed it open. There was no room but a long spiral staircase that went down. This was different. Everything was white. The stairs, the walls if there were any.

"Do you hear that?" asked Rapha looking at Caleb.

"Yes."

"That's the sound the green fire balls made at the Village of Fences," replied Rapha

"And the smell," said Wah'li'si.

"The smell of rotting worms, and dirty little demons!" replied Christopher.

Caleb led the way through the door and down the stairs saying, "Let's fine Eli'Zur."

The staircase seemed to go on and on. Just when they thought it wasn't going to end, it did. About fifty feet in front of them was one red door.

"Come on," said Caleb as he went toward the door. As soon as they reached the door, Caleb opened it. Inside in the middle of the room was Eli'Zur, strapped to a table by ankles and wrist. Above was swinging pendulum. It was now only inches from slicing his stomach wide open. Eli'Zur looked over at them and said, "Caleb!"

"Move quickly," said Caleb as Logan and Christopher went down by Eli' Zur's feet. Caleb and Rapha stood by his wrists.

"Lift up your right hands toward Heaven." When they did, Caleb said, "Oh Timeless-One, empower us." At that moment Caleb and the others brought their hands down holding a Spirit sword and in one motion struck the straps that bound Eli'Zur to the table. Eli'Zur rolled off the table just before the blade could touch him. Christopher went over to help Eli'Zur off the floor and said, "Cut it kind of close, huh?"

"Christopher!" scolded Wah'li'si.

"Funny, very funny," said Eli'Zur sarcastically. Caleb and Eli'Zur quickly hugged.

"Thanks Caleb," said Eli'Zur.

"It's alright," replied Caleb.

"Look, another door," said Logan.

"It's the only one here too," said Rapha.

"It's also black," said Caleb.

As they got closer to the door it began opening slowly on its own. When they went through the door, it shut and vanished behind them. Now, they stood in the middle of a large room. The floor was black, and they were standing within a silver circle that was etched in it. In front of them was a court bench that was high off the ground. An inverted pentagram hung above it. Behind them they could hear whispers and laughing so they turned around. What they saw was a room full of hideous looking demons.

Then a hollow gong rang loudly six times. Afterward three brightly dressed men came from behind a curtain to the left of the room and walked up and sat down behind the court bench. The man in the middle took the mallet in his hand and struck the bench saying, "Court is now in session."

"So, Mr. Caleb, I trust you had fun getting here. I know I did," said the man in the middle.

"Are you the littlest of gods?" demanded Caleb.

"Oh no, no. He won't be joining us today. No," said the man in the middle.

"Coward!" said Christopher.

Caleb looked at the others and said, "No more words."

The man in the middle spoke saying, "My name is Cancer. To my right is Lust and to my left is Reprobate." Cancer leaned over and whispered to Lust, then leaned over and whispered to Reprobate.

Cancer put his hands on the bench and said, "Caleb, High Priest, you and your regime are guilty of many war crimes including murder, torture, and illegal entry on sacred grounds. How do you plead?"

Caleb nor the others said a word. "Not talking? That reminds me of another man that kept silent. We killed him anyway," said Cancer.

"I say they are guilty," said Lust.

"Guilty," said Reprobate.

"Alright! Guess what- you're guilty!" Cancer said with his teeth showing.

"The game is over!" said Caleb as he walked closer to the bench.

"Get back to your circle!" yelled Cancer.

"I am not subject to you!" said Caleb with authority. "Look upon us with eyes wide open. Open your eyes and see who you are up against," continued Caleb. There was a flash of white light, and Caleb and the regime was seen in the flesh as they are seen in the spirit, covered in the blood of the Lamb. The demons in the courtroom started exploding and screaming in pain as they looked upon the blood.

"The blood of the Lamb heals," said Wah'li'si softly.

"Silence!" yelled Cancer.

"The blood of the Lamb reveals," said Logan in a whisper.

"Silence!" yelled Cancer again as he stood to his feet.

"What is the matter, Cancer? Why don't you call on your god? Maybe he can help?" said Caleb sarcastically.

"The blood of the Lamb delivers," said Rapha quietly, but it echoed in Cancer's ears.

"Satan where are you?" yelled Cancer. The courtroom thundered and lightening struck the demons as they tried to run.

"The blood of the Lamb judges the wicked," said Eli'Zur very softly. Blood began dripping from the ceiling, falling on Caleb and the others. As it landed on Caleb and his regime, they became more at peace and refreshed. But as the blood hit the demons it was as if acid was landing on them, and they cried out in agony as they melted.

"The blood of the Lamb cleanses the universe of all evil," said Christopher with a peace in his voice. The screams of the demons as they were being destroyed pierced Cancer's being and made him cringe.

"Leave this place, now!" screamed Cancer. "Not until you die," said Caleb. Just then lightning struck Cancer, Lust and Reprobate. Then they were no more. The room was empty and quiet.

"Awesome," said Christopher.

Caleb walked back to the others and said, "Lift up holy hands." They all lifted their hands, palms up. Then Caleb said,

"Oh Timeless-One
Again, you delivered us.
Again, You came to our rescue.

"You carried us.
You sheltered our souls.
And cleansed us in your blood.

Full of power, honor, and glory.
Amen."

Everyone saying, "Amen."

When they brought their hands down and opened their eyes, they were in the Temple Yard back at High Rock. Then Wah'li'si led them in a time of praise and worship.

People gathered in the Temple yard. Caleb sat down and told everyone of their adventure.

To be continued . . .

13

THE PSALMUS

"Words of the wise, spoken quietly, should be heard. Rather than the shout of a ruler of fools."

Ecclesiastes 9:17 NKJV

Full of the fire of the Timeless-One, and with complete wisdom and understanding of the Holy Verses, the man of great age known simply as The Psalmus spoke to Caleb saying,

"Let every breath you take,
Every word you speak.
Every line you pen,
Let every heartbeat,
Every wink of the eye,
Every word uttered.
Let every action and reaction.
Be for the Lord Most High."

Caleb sat there on the ground with his legs crossed in silence. Night had fallen as they sat by the stream next to the fire. The moonlight bouncing off the waves of the water and the sound of the crackling wood in the fire made the moment even more special. For whenever Caleb speaks with the Psalmus, Caleb is encouraged and uplifted in spirit.

Seated on a large log, the Psalmus takes a twig in his hand and leaned over and stirred the fire. Burning embers flew through the night sky disappearing to be replaced by the fireflies. Then he looked at Caleb and spoke once again saying:

"When the littlest of gods raises his sword of hate against you,

And spews his blackened fire from his eyes to blind you,

Shout the Word! Cry out the Name! Lift your heel,

And crush his head! The Lord Your God is with you!"

Caleb lifted his hands in the air and with a smile on his face said,

"Blessed is the Lord Most High,

Words from the Word through a willing vessel.

Amen."

All was quiet when Caleb looked across the fire to the Psalmus and with sadness in his voice he said,

"Psalmus, secret ears long to hear. Hidden hearts long to be filled. Anxious eyes yearn to see, and lonely lips hunger to praise."

"As mourning is turned to praises and night is turned today, the hungry shall be filled, and the dying shall be saved," replied the Psalmus.

"Let it be so. Amen," said Caleb.

As they sat there with only the campfire, the moon and stars to light the evening the Word appeared before them, sitting with them around the fire. Caleb and the Psalmus fell back as dead.

"Arise," said the Word.

"Caleb and the Psalmus sat up and said, "Holy, Holy, Holy is the Commander of the Lord and the King that forever reigns.

The Word, sitting between them reached out with both hands and touched their shoulders, smiled and said, "Peace to you. The Father is pleased with the words that proceed from your mouths and from your hearts." The Word continued speaking saying.

"The Son shines on the wicked and the righteous, yet the wicked do not see it."

"The Spirit moves across the land like a mighty whirlwind.

"The Righteous stand in the midst of it and say, 'Fill us, fill us.'

"The wicked runs and hides in caves."

Then the Word reached His hand into the fire and pulled out a flame. He held His hand out with palms up. The flame danced on His hand and neither burned Him nor went out. Then he said, "As the fire moves like a hurricane and purifies all it touches, the wicked crawl under rocks for cover. The righteous say 'Consume us.'"

The Psalmus raised his right hand and said, "Mysteries revealed, secrets known, words from the Word, and knowledge from the All Knowing."

Then Caleb put his head down and lifted both hands and said, "Oh, You have blessed us indeed and enriched our souls."

The Word looked at Caleb with His eyes full of love and penetrating fire and said, "Caleb."

Caleb didn't look up but said, "Yes, Lord."

"Until the days are complete," said the Word, "Where will you be?"

Caleb answered, "Here, serving You."

Again, the Word said, "As the day draws nearer, where will you be?"

Caleb answered, "Here on this earth serving only You."

The Word questioned again, "Tell me, when the day of completeness arrives, then what?"

Keeping his head down and not looking up Caleb answered saying, "To be transformed and leave this place to be where you are."

The Word smiled. When he smiled, his eyes smiled with Him and He said, "Oh Caleb. I love you. When the day comes you will, you shall be with me forever."

The Word looked over at the Psalmus and said, "Great Psalmus, you have served the Eternal Kingdom well. By inspiration you have penned great songs and poems that uplifted many hearts. Your example has influenced all who watch you. And you have mentored a great warrior high priest. Psalmus, you are complete. This day you will be transformed."

The Psalmus lifted his hands and did not look upon the Word. Tears flowed down his face as he said, "Oh, how I longed for this day and dreamed of this hour to be transformed and taken to the Golden City. Oh, my heart is dancing. Holy, holy, holy." The Psalmus brought his hands down and brought them together and held them to his chest. Then he sat quietly smiling.

Caleb rejoiced in his heart for the Psalmus and at the same time was saddened for he felt he would deeply miss him.

"Caleb," said the Word. "Caleb, look at me."

"I cannot Lord," replied Caleb.

"Yes, you can," said the Word. "You will not die."

Caleb looked up at the Word very slowly. When he saw His face, the Word was illuminating a soft white glow, and had a big smile on His face. Caleb trembled and said, "Holy."

"You're ok Caleb," said the Word as he reached over and touched his shoulder. "It is time he has finished his work," said the Lord. "Your time is coming and when it comes, I personally will come and bring you home as I did the Psalmus."

"Holy is the Lord," proclaimed Caleb.

The Word stood to His feet and said, "It is time." Then Caleb and the Psalmus stood.

"Come," said the Word to the Psalmus.

"Lord," said the Psalmus, "May I speak with Caleb before we go?"

The Word smiled and motioned with His head to go ahead. The Psalmus walked over to Caleb and said, "Before the foundations of the galaxies were laid, The Timeless-One looked across time and saw you and He smiled."

"I will miss you Psalmus," said Caleb as he reached over and hugged him.

"Hey, I'm going to the Golden City," assured the Psalmus. Then he turned and walked toward the Word. Before he reached Him, a fiery whirlwind started descending from the sky with a roar. The Psalmus stopped and turned around. With a loud voice and outstretched arms, he spoke to Caleb saying, "Caleb. Warrior. High Priest! Slayer of demons! Friend of God!"

Just then the fiery whirlwind came upon all three of them with a very loud roar. Caleb stood within the twisting blaze worshipping God.

After about three minutes, the whirlwind lifted taking the Word and the Psalmus leaving Caleb in full worship and not one hair on his head burned. Then he sang a song of praise,

"Oh, Holy One, You ride the ancient skies,

You fill my being with fire,

I look to the heavens,

And wait for Your triumphant return."

Caleb went down to the Temple Yard and called everyone together. He told of what happened to the Psalmus and of the Word and the whirlwind. Then Wah'li'si and Ovation led everyone in praise and worship.

To be continued…

14

PORTAL

For we do not wrestle against flesh and blood, but against principalities, against powers, against the rulers of the darkness of this age, against spiritual hosts of wickedness in the heavenly places.

(Ephesians 6:12 NKJV)

Land Enchant

In a dimly lit room, the magician stood in a black hooded robe at his podium. The podium stood in the middle of the room, in the middle of a circle of protection that was drawn on the floor. This was his enchanted room, and this was where he did his conjuring and spellcasting. Looking down into his Grimoire, his "Book of Shadows", he slowly turned the well-used pages that have become discolored, and the edges worn. He then stopped on page 136; this was his evocation he named, "The Binding of Legion".

This man has spent the last twenty years of his life perfecting and strengthening his darkened powers. He has studied all forms of the black arts including, Magick, Witchcraft, Alchemy and even the worship of the littlest of gods himself. Although he was only thirty-eight years of age, he looked about sixty, for all the evil that he has consumed, has taken a toll on his body. Now, he feels that he is the one who is in control, that he is the one full of power and full of all knowledge of the occult. Now, he will conjure the ancient and prevailing one, the one that is many, Legion.

The circle of protection began making an electrifying humming sound, and then a blue light surrounded the circle like a bubble. This is a force field that protects everyone and everything that is within the circle from harm, and from the evil that is being evoked. The man raised his arms, holding a magic wand in his right hand; he began to recite his incantation, "I call thee ancient one who is many! I call thee, Legion to stand before me! I summon thee and bind thee for my service. I, thy master demand thee to appear before me and bow and swear allegiance! Come forth!" Just then the room began to shake violently. Candles, mirrors and magick books fell to the floor. The blue protective bubble had turned blood red, (this has never happened before). The magician held on to the podium with his left hand, trying not to fall, while attempting to evoke Legion and holding the wand high. Then outside the bubble a green circular light appeared hovering about six feet off the floor. It was about five feet in diameter. With a loud sucking sound, the center of the light collapsed, and it became a kind of tunnel or hole in midair. Then with a loud roar a grayish green hand came through the tunnel and out of the opening flying towards the magician. When it came to the protective bubble, the bubble shattered with a loud pop into thousands of pieces and vanished. The hand grabbed the magic wand and took it back in the tunnel with it. The magician fell to the floor and heard a deep and evil voice come from the tunnel that said, "The servant will never be greater than the master! We are through with you!" And with that the green tunnel vanished, the room stopped shaking and the magician tried to catch his breath while still on the floor. Then he passed out.

When the magician came to, it was morning, he stood to his feet and began straightening up his room when he noticed his athame; (black handled enchanted knife) was missing. He began to search frantically for it, but it was nowhere to be found. Then he thought to himself, "It too was taken through the portal to the place where magick is born and where the blackest of power is created, the dimension of the Stygian Flame." As he walked by the large mirror that hung by the door, he heard a loud sucking sound and then a pop come from the mirror. He quickly turned and looked, the frame of the mirror was there, but inside the frame was the green portal. Then from within the portal came a voice growling, "Magic man, we're coming for you!" Then the voice turned into a sound of a multitude roaring, "I said I'm coming for you!" Just then greyish green hands with black nails that looked like claws reached through the portal and grabbed hold of the sides of the mirror frame and pulled it apart. Then a hideous evil demonic head came through growling. It had pure black eyes, a flat nose and a large mouth with black razor-sharp teeth. The magician stumbled backward in shock. With one hand the demon reached for the magician and missed. The magician quickly grabbed an inverted crucifix from the wall and held it right side up in front of him. The demon growled, "You are so naïve!" The demon grabbed the crucifix out of the magician's hand and said with the sound of a multitude, "I am against you! I am going to bring you to the Stygian Flame that never goes out! We will feed on your flesh! You will never die, and I will always hunger!" When the demon finished speaking, he vanished as did the portal and the crucifix. The mirror was in pieces, but the wall behind it was not disturbed. The magician grabbed his book of shadows, his pouch of magic crystal dust and fled the house, not knowing where he was going.

At High Rock, (that same morning)

"You can't do it like that." said Logan. "Yes, I can." replied Christopher. "No, you can't!" demanded Logan. "Yes, I can!" claimed Christopher.

Caleb and Wah'li'si sat under the shade tree, along with Saleah, Zoe and Caleb's wolves, watching Christopher and Logan disagree on how to tie a tail on a kite for little Gabe and Ben. The two boys just stood there patiently. "It will never hold man." said Logan. "It will hold!" affirmed Christopher. Suddenly, a mighty rushing wind came in from the east. Christopher grabbed the boys and said, "Get inside." The boys ran into the Hall of Visions. Logan and Christopher struggled to remain standing. Caleb and Wah'li'si held on to the wolves tightly. The wind roared, as it bent the trees and violently blew dust and leaves in the air. Then out of the east sky a fiery chariot drawn by four horses of blue flames descended from the sky with a loud growl like many lions. The fiery horse drawn chariot landed in the street between Caleb and Wah'li'si, and Logan and Christopher. No one was driving the chariot, although one of the horses turned its head towards Caleb and said with a growling roar, "All of you get in!" "That just didn't happen!" demanded Christopher. Then another horse turned his head toward Christopher and Logan and growled, "There's no time to waste! Get in!" As they all climbed in the chariot Christopher said excitedly, "Okay, okay, climbing in!" Caleb's wolves jumped in as well. Gabe and Ben watched in amazement as the fiery horse drawn chariot flew off with Caleb and the rest inside.

As they flew off into the sky, a glittering silver, circular object appeared in the sky. The horses headed straight towards it, and just before they reached it, the center collapsed making a tunnel. The horses flew into it, as they did, the tunnel disappeared. The chariot flew through the tunnel like lightening. As they flew, multicolored lights surrounded them as did the sound of heavenly, angelic singing and the indescribable sound of loud music.

The trip took just minutes, but when they came out the other side, they were in a very strange place. Unlike any place they have ever seen. As they came down out of the sky, they could see mountains that were pure black, trees that looked like shadows. No grass, no leaves. There was a lake; it too was black as coal.

Land Enchant: The Holy Regime

The horses landed in the middle of what looked like a deserted village, it too was dark and gray. No color anywhere. When the chariot came to a stop, they all got out. One of the horses turned to Caleb and said with a growl, "Find him! Find him, before they do!" "Find who?" asked Caleb. "The Timeless-One wants you to bring the magic man into the fold. You must find him! They are after him!" growled the horse. "Who is the "magic man"? And who's after him?" asked Caleb. The horse didn't answer but flew off. As the chariot flew off, another horse roared, saying, "we will return in three days! Be here with him!" Christopher looked up at the horses, cupped his hands by his mouth and yelled, "Who!" They watched as the chariot disappeared into the tunnel.

"Where are we?" asked Saleah. "I don't know." answered Caleb. "So," said Christopher as he started pacing and waving his hands around, "We don't know where we are. We don't know who we are going to look for. And we don't who is after him." He stopped and looked at everyone and said, "Right?" "Christopher, Tohinusdv." Assured Wah'li'si in her native tongue (Tohinusdv means, "calm"). "Let's look around. Maybe we can find a clue of where we're at." said Logan. "Good idea." said Caleb. "But first," he continued, "let's heart-link to the Timeless-One." They all lifted their hands, palms up and then tilted their heads back looking up as Caleb led them in the heart-link saying,

"Oh, Timeless-One
You are the Aleph and the Tav, The Alpha and Omega
The Beginning and the end
And only You have seen both.
Great and powerful are You Oh, Timeless-One
Guide our every step."

Caleb walked over behind Zoe and Saleah and put his hands on their shoulders and said, "The village isn't very big so, let's split up into pairs and look around. We'll meet back here in one hour, okay?" Everyone agreed. Christopher and Logan went toward the east. Saleah and Zoe took one of Caleb's wolves and went to the west end of town. Caleb and Wah'li'si went to the north end of town and his other wolf followed.

Land Enchant: Magic Man

The magic man ran from his house with all his might. He ran for about an hour when he came to the edge of, Nightmare Woods. He stopped there at the edge to catch his breath. He had never feared these woods before, but now something has changed. Many years ago, he cursed these woods with a spell of fear. So, when all who enter the woods, their deepest fears come to life. Now, he felt, for the first time, anxiety about entering the woods, but it was the quickest way to Angelick Village, the dwelling of the Light Divines, the place of the purest white magic. With his, "Book of Shadows" under his arm, he took a deep breath and said to himself, "Here we go!" He took off, running as fast as he could again, brushing limbs and bushes out of the way with his free hand, and jumping over logs and rocks, trying to get to the other side of the woods as fast as he could.

Then, from either side of him he could hear a loud, multitude of evil voices chanting, "Run, run, run, run." This went on for about half an hour, nonstop. Then, a streak of green light flew by him on the right, passed him and stopped ten feet in front of the magic man. The man stopped running and tripped and almost fell into the green light. The man was just inches away from the light, when from within it he heard the sucking sound then, the loud pop. The center collapsed and from within the portal came the voices of Legion, "Magic man!" they snarled, "You cannot run from me!" The portal was acting like some kind of vacuum, pulling the magic man towards it. Magic man grabbed a limb of a nearby tree.

He held on as tight as he could, as his feet kept sliding towards the portal. "Let go!" they growled, "It's just a matter of time before you will be kneeling at the Stygian Flame!" The magic man's feet were now off the ground and being pulled by the vacuum of the portal. Trying to hang on with one hand, he dropped his "Book of Shadows". It fell to the ground face up, opened to a spell called, "The Restraining." He began to recite the spell at the top of his

lungs, for the sound of the vacuum of the portal was thundering loud, "Be ye gone! Be ye lost! Go ye far! Restrain . . . ye . . . must!" At that instant the portal closed and vanished, and the magic man fell to the ground. He laid there for a second to catch his breath, and then he got up dust his clothes off, grabbed his book and ran off again.

Land Enchant: Holy Regime

As Caleb and the others searched the village, it appeared to be deserted. Saleah and Zoe came upon the village square and in the middle was statue of a man with wings and a halo. "Let's go take a look." Zoe said to Saleah. As they walked over, they saw that the statue was about nine feet tall and was holding a large book. "What does it say on the book, Zoe?" asked Saleah. "It . . . says . . . ", Zoe squinting to make it out, for the statue too was gray and dark, "Magick of the Light, Light of the Magick." "What does that mean?" asked Saleah. "White magic, maybe?" answered Zoe. "Maybe." said Saleah. "Let's keep looking." said Zoe. "Yeah, let's go." answered Saleah. "Come, Wah'ya." said Zoe calling the wolf.

"Hey, check this out!" Christopher said excitedly. "What's that?" answered Logan as he walked over to where Christopher was at. "Look at the wall, man!" demanded Christopher. Logan and Christopher were standing on the sidewalk under an awning just outside of a store. "What about the wall?" asked Logan. "Just watch. Wait for it." Christopher replied. Logan stood there a few seconds looking at the wall and asked, "What am I looking . . . "Just then an image of a winged man moved within the wall.

The wall was black as coal and the image was slightly lighter in shade. Logan jumped back and yelled, "Whoa! Did you see that?!" "Look! Another one!" pointed Christopher. "How?" asked Logan. Just then another image moved and turned to look at Christopher and Logan. The image opened his mouth to speak, but Christopher and Logan could not hear him. "He sees us!" said Logan. "What's he doing?" asked Christopher. The image was pointing to the statue in the town square. "He's pointing at something." said Christopher. Logan and Christopher looked around and then Logan said, "Looks like he's pointing at the village square." "Yeah, let's check it out." replied Christopher.

As Logan and Christopher were making their way to the town square Caleb and Wah'li'si were walking up stairs to what looked like a temple. The temple was as black as the other buildings. The double doors in front were about thirteen feet tall with engravings on them. "Look at these markings on the doors Caleb." said Wah'li'si. "I've, seen these before." Caleb explained. Pointing at the engravings, Caleb continued, "The inverted star and the inverted cross, I saw these symbols at Mr. Wizards dwelling." Then pointing at another engraving that took up the whole left door, Caleb said, "And this, this is Baphomet (Baphomet has the appearance of man with goat legs and a goat's head with a flame of fire between the horns). I met him on the way to meet Mr. Wizard. The Timeless-One destroyed him, right before my eyes." "The littlest of gods, in the end, is," Wah'li'si gestured with a wave of her right hand and said in her native tongue, "Utloyi Nigvnada." (This means, "The same everywhere".) Caleb opened the doors; it was pitch-black inside. They stepped inside, and Caleb's wolf followed them in. Once through, the doors slammed shut, and at that instant the temple was brightly illuminated. Everything inside was white and brilliant, sparkling crystal was everywhere. Caleb's wolf started growling and the fur on his back rose. Caleb reached down and patted his head and said, "Hush, Neshoba it is alright." Neshoba quieted down, but kept his eyes and head moving, looking around. "So . . . this is different, ay?" questioned Wah'li'si. "Quite." answered Caleb.

Caleb and Wah'li'si stood, looking at what looked like huge throne room. The throne itself was white and sat on a platform at the front of the room, with thirteen steps going up to it. All along the white walls were white candles and engravings, engravings of inverted stars, inverted crosses, signs of the zodiac and the tarot. In the center of the room was a very large red circle on the white floor with a red five-pointed star inside it. The points of the star touched the edge of the circle, and at each point of the star was a crystal candle stand with a single lit white candle. Caleb and Wah'li'si began to step down into the throne room when a man that resembled an angel appeared standing by the throne.

The man stood about nine feet tall and wore a white robe that went down to his feet with a red sash about his waist. He had large white angelic wings and shoulder length straight white hair. He appeared to be about thirty years of age. "Don't come any farther!" he said with a booming voice that echoed in the empty throne room. Caleb and Wah'li'si stopped. Caleb didn't have a chance to say anything when the man continued speaking, saying, "The magick you seek, is not here." The man stretched out his wings and lifted himself off the floor and continued, "Seek your magick in the circle of the square." And at that instant with a swishing sound the man vanished. The room went pitch black and Caleb said, "Time to leave!" Caleb and Wah'li'si turned and felt for the door, opened it and left. Once outside Wah'li'si questioned, "Seek your magick in the circle of the square?" "Circle of the square." Caleb pondered. "The center of a town is sometimes called a square." Calcb continued. "Let's go." Replied Wah'li'si.

Saleah and Zoe had walked a few yards away from the village square, when up out of the ground, right in front of them appeared, a pure black wolf with blood red eyes and large sharp black teeth. Wah'ya, Caleb's wolf got between Saleah and Zoe and the wolf. The hair on the neck of Wah'ya was standing up and he was showing his teeth and growling. "Wah'ya!" yelled Saleah as she reached for him. Zoe grabbed Saleah by the arm and demanded,

"No, Saleah!" The black wolf spoke and said with a growl, "No farther!" The black wolf paced back and forth as Wah'ya watched his every move.

"The center of the middle," the wolf continued, "within the four sides of the circle is where you will find your magick! Go back!" Then with a swishing sound the wolf vanished back down into the earth. "Okay, that was a little unexpected." said Zoe. "Good boy, Wah'ya." said Saleah as she bent down and hugged him. "The center of the middle?" questioned Zoe. "And four sides of the circle?" replied Saleah. "He said, 'Go back'." said Zoe. "Go back where?" asked Saleah. Then they both said together, "The town square!" "Let's go." said Saleah.

Land Enchant: Magic Man

As the magic man continued running through Nightmare Woods, he could hear the sound of many beating hearts echoing in his ears. Then without warning a large tree moved in front of him, the man stumbled and fell. Before he could get up three more trees moved in and surrounded him. The man stood to his feet, clutching his "Book of Shadows"; he quickly turned back and forth looking at the trees. Then the trees spoke in unison saying in a wicked and evil whisper, "Hand . . . over . . . the . . . book!" "I will not!" shouted the man as he held the book even tighter. Just then the tree to the man's right reached one of its branches out and it became an arm and hand; it swung at the man and missed. The man fell and rolled on the ground and quickly stood to his feet, never loosening his grip on the book. The trees now had blood red eyes and large mouths with huge fangs. The trees started moving towards the man closing the circle around him. "We . . . are . . . going . . . to . . . take . . . the . . . book . . . then . . . eat . . . your . . . flesh!" the trees whispered in unison as they continued moving closer to the man. The magic man reached into his magic pouch he had hanging around his neck and pulled some of his magic crystal dust out and said, "From the ground thee emerged.

Into thin air thou goest!" Then the man held the dust up to his mouth, and then he spun around in a circle blowing the dust at the trees.

As the dust filled the air and touched the trees, the trees instantly disintegrated with the sound of crackling wood. The ashes fell to the ground, then instantly shout up in the air and disappeared.

The man took off running again, and in about twenty minutes he could see the edge of the woods. When, directly in front of him at the edge of the woods, the portal appeared. The magic man instantly came to a stop. From within the portal came the sounds of voices crying out in pain and anguish, then the voice of Legion, "We are Legion! I am here!" Then more screams of people in pain came from the portal. "Stay away from me!" yelled the magic man. "I am your master! Be gone!" magic man commanded.

The portal was not acting like a vacuum this time but began humming, like it was full of electricity, when suddenly three creatures leaped out of the portal. They appeared to be men wearing red hooded robes with black sashes about their waists. Their faces were not visible, only their dark glowing green eyes and long stringy black hair hanging out from under their hoods. The creatures were about six feet tall but could not stand upright. They moved almost ape-like circling the man. Then one spoke in a raspy demonic voice, "I am Mephistopheles, and these are Lucifuge and Asmodeus. Yes, yes. We are the crown princes of hell! Yes, yes." Breathing heavily, they circled the man as he moved back and forth trying to watch them all. "Be gone!" the man demanded. "Go, before I send you far beyond the Stygian Flame!" "You are not Priest Caleb!" the creature scoffed. Then, one of the creatures threw a ball of fire at the man. The man lifted his book of shadows just in time for the ball of fire to hit it and explode, leaving him unharmed. Mephistopheles said, "You're coming with us to Legion!" Just then, all three creatures lifted their claw-like hands above their heads. Then all three creatures spoke in unison, "A web of lies, and a web of cries. Down to the Stygian Flame, down to the Stygian pain!" As Mephistopheles was speaking, out of the fingertips of the three creatures came glowing green lights, stretching up and connecting with each of the other light strings, forming a giant web, surrounding the man.

The man was paralyzed and was unable to speak. "Come to me, Bryan. Who once was the great man of magick and ruler of demons." mocked Legion. The three creatures dragged Bryan in the web towards the portal, when an intensely white bright light shown down from the sky on the entire area. The portal, the three creatures and Bryan were all within the light. Then out of the light came the thundering voice of the Timeless-One, "He's Mine!" Then what looked like red laser beams came out of the sky and struck the web. The web dissolved with the sound of sizzling.

Then another laser struck each creature as they tried to run back to the portal, they exploded with a loud shriek. As Bryan lay on the ground, he saw another laser come from the sky towards the portal, just before the laser reached it, the portal vanished. Now, Bryan did not hear the voice of the Timeless-One speak, but he knew the lights were not of this world. He got up and ran to the edge of the woods. He stopped just outside the woods to catch his breath, he looked, and afar off, he could see Angelick Village. He thought, "I'm almost there." He started walking this time to the village.

Land Enchant – Angelick Village The Holy Regime

They all arrived at the village square at the same time. "Well, fancy meeting all you here." joking Christopher as he and Logan walked up. "This is a strange, strange place, Caleb." said Zoe. "That's an understatement." replied Christopher. Caleb walked toward the statue and said, "It looks like everything points to this spot." "Yes, the man said, 'The circle of the square.'" explained Wah'li'si. "And the wolf said," Replied Saleah, "the center of the middle." "The wolf said?" asked Christopher. "Get used to it Christopher." said Logan, putting his hand on his shoulder. "Caleb," said Wah'li'si, "This statue looks like the man in the temple." "You're right, it does." replied Caleb. Then Caleb read what was on the book the statue was holding, "Magick of the Light, Light of the Magick." "Unegah magick."

Wah'li'si replied, meaning "white magick". "Caleb," Saleah asked, "is there really any such thing as Unegah magick?" "No, Saleah," replied Caleb, "evil is evil, and magick is magick. The littlest of gods is the father of evil, and magick is a snare to draw the innocent into his wicked grip."

"Okay," asked Logan, "we are looking for the circle of the square and the center of the middle, right?" He said as he started walking around the statue, looking at the ground. "Hey, guys," asked Christopher, "what does this have to do with whom we're supposed to be looking for?" "I don't know Christopher," answered Caleb, "but, we have to follow the leads." "But" Christopher replied, "what if the leads lead us into a trap?" "The Timeless-One is with us, right Caleb?" asked Zoe. "Yes, most assuredly He is Zoe." They all began walking around the square looking for, 'something' not knowing what. Then Wah'li'si called Caleb over to where she was, "Caleb, over here!" Caleb went over to where Wah'li'si was, and the others came over as well. "What is it?" asked Caleb. Wah'li'si had climbed up on the back of a park bench, holding herself steady by holding on to a nearby tree. "Is that safe?" asked Christopher. Waving her hand around in a circular motion Wah'li'si said, "**Itsula Gadogv Hawiniditlv**." Meaning, "We stand within." As they all turned around, looking they could see a circle on the ground that went around the inner edge of the town square. The circles edge was about three feet wide, with symbols within it, spaced out every six feet. The symbols included pentagrams, runes, astrological signs and others. Then Wah'li'si said while still standing on the back of the bench, "Look at the sidewalks." As they looked, they noticed the sidewalks made a perfect pentagram, touching the edge of the circle and crossing in the center, the statue was in the middle of the pentagram. "The town square," Caleb explained, "is the town's ceremonial site." "Yeah, and we're standing in the middle of it." replied Christopher. As Caleb started to help Wah'li'si down off the back of the bench the ground started to shake. Caleb's wolves, Wah'ya and Neshoba started growling at the statue, while the outer ring of the circle started turning counterclockwise and glowing green it began making a humming sound.

They all stood there, watching the ring turn. "Caleb?" said Saleah. Just then, the statue started spinning clockwise very rapidly. Then, with a loud pop, the statue fell through the ground with much speed. In its place was a hole in the ground with green light shining out of it. From within the hole came a low humming sound, different from that the ring was making. Mingled with the humming was the sound of people in anguish and pain, yelling and screaming. Then, from within all that noise, the voice of evil emerged with the sound of a multitude of speaking in unison, "I am Legion! Be gone from this place! Go now, and you may live! Stay and die!" At that instant the hole was sealed up with dirt and the ring stopped turning.

"Someone or something doesn't want us here!" said Zoe excitedly. "That hole was that . . ." said Logan as Caleb interrupts and said, "That was a portal, a portal to another dimension." "Do I want to know what dimension? Or do I know?" asked Christopher. Caleb had walked over to where the portal appeared, he turned and looked at the others and explained, "It is a portal that leads directly to the Stygian Kingdom ruled by Legion." "Legion from the Holy Scriptures?" asked Wah'li'si. "The very same." answered Caleb. "Legion is an army, man!" replied Christopher with much emotion. "All is well, guys." affirmed Caleb. "Dude, we don't even have our Spirit Swords!" explained Christopher. "The Timeless-One came here before us. Everything is set in place, just as it should be." Explained Caleb, then he motioned for everyone to come in close and he said, "Let us heart-link with the Timeless-One." So, they all lifted their hands and tilted the heads back, facing the sky as Caleb lead them in heart-linking,

"Oh, Timeless-One,
You are the Holy One,

You are the True One,
You are the Only One."

When they were through, they all felt energized and empowered by the Timeless-One. "Now, what do we do?" asked Saleah.

"We wait, but while we wait, let us see if we can see why this place seems to be deserted." replied Caleb. "But it's not deserted. The people are **in** the walls." answered Christopher. "In the walls?" asked Zoe. "Yes, they are alive and moving **within** the walls of the buildings." explained Christopher. "Show us." said Caleb.

Land Enchant –
Between Angelick Village and Nightmare Woods
Bryan the Magic Man

As Bryan walked, he was about halfway between Nightmare Woods and Angelick Village when a door came down from the sky with lightning speed. The door landed upright directly in front of him kicking up dust. The door was solid metallic black. Bryan stopped and looked at the door for a second and said, "I don't think so!" He turned to the left to go around it when another door slammed down in front of him, blocking his way. Then he quickly spun around to go the opposite way when two more doors slammed down, enclosing him in. He quickly opened his "Book of Shadows" searching for a spell to remove the doors when, suddenly, he could hear knocking on the other side of the doors. At first, it was soft, then as he searched the book the knocking became louder and louder, to the point of pounding. Then the doorknobs started shaking and turning back and forth. Bryan stopped at a page and started reciting a spell, "Doors to be opened, doors to be shut. Doors . . ." Before he could finish the spell, loud and evil, demonic voices came from behind the doors mocking, they said, "Open the doors Bryan, great and powerful magic man!" Bryan started shouting his spell, "Doors to be opened, doors to be . . ." Just then the doors vanished. One by one the doors disappeared, leaving only the doorframes. And what he saw, he could not believe.

Behind the first door he saw to his amazement, was Baphomet, sitting cross-legged on nothing. He was floating in mid-air, surrounded by nothing but, black empty space. Baphomet opened his mouth and lava spewed out and he said in an evil, slow and distorted voice, "You're dead, magic man!" He turned quickly and inside the next door was a lake of fire and blood.

As far as he could see was fire mingled with blood. He turned again and inside the next door was thousands and thousands of people standing motionless, paralyzed in a valley made of black, volcanic rock. All they could do is scream at the top of their lungs in pain as demons tormented them with the ripping of their flesh, the gouging of their eyes and pouring flaming worms on their heads. Bryan held his stomach and turned, stumbling to the next door sick and disturbed. As he looked inside the last door, he couldn't believe his eyes. He started shaking his head and saying, "No, no, no!" What he saw was he himself standing over a man that was lying on a long wood post with a crossbeam at the shoulders. The man had been brutally beaten to near death. The man lay there with arms stretched out on the crossbeam as his blood covered the wood and dripped onto the ground. Bryan saw as he himself placed his foot on one of the man's hands, then he took a large nail and put it on the man's wrist. As Bryan took a large hammer in his other hand and held it above his head ready to drive the nail into the wrist of the man, he looked over his shoulder with an evil grin at himself standing outside the door. Bryan swung the hammer down on the nail, driving it into the man's wrist and into the wood. As the man screamed in pain, he lifted his head and looked at Bryan who stood on the outside of the door and said, "This is for you." In disbelief Bryan shook his head and said, "What?" Then the doorframes fell back on the ground and vanished. Bryan clutched his "Book of Shadows" and held it against his chest and said, "I'll sort this out at Angelick Village." Then he headed for the village once again.

Land Enchant – Angelick Village
The Holy Regime

They walked to a building; it had an awning out front with a sign on it that read, "The Recipes". "For some reason," Christopher said, "I don't think they're talking about food." No one replied. Then he said waving his hands about, "Anyone? Anyone?" Zoe punched him in the arm and said, "Hush!" Saleah was walking by Zoe and high-fived her. "Okay, okay!" replied Christopher as he rubbed his arm. They all lined up facing the building. "Now what?" asked Saleah. "Just wait." answered Logan. Just then a man with wings appeared in the wall, walking from one end of the building to the other. They all took a step back. "Caleb, what do you think?" asked Wah'li'si. "This magick came from another dimension. This is not earth born." answered Caleb. "What do you mean, Caleb, another dimension?" asked Zoe.

Caleb turned and stepped off the sidewalk, then he turned back around and faced Wah'li'si and the rest and explained, "A magician, witch or wizard did not do this to this village. The power at work here comes from the dimension of 'The Outer Darkness'. Although, this village **did** practice a form of magick, this we know by all the signs, they did not do . . . this." "Outer Darkness?" questioned Logan. "When Legion spoke to us from the portal, we could hear the voices of thousands upon thousands of people crying out in anguish and pain." Caleb explained. "And" continued Caleb, "Legion, he himself is from the very pit of hell." "But why do this to your own followers, and what does this have to do with the person we're looking for?" asked Christopher. "Maybe," said Wah'li'si, "the person we are looking for isn't here yet. And maybe this person needed the help from the people of this village, and Legion put a stop to it happening." Then Caleb said, "Let us heart-link to the Timeless-One for wisdom and understanding . . . come." They all gathered around in a circle and lifted their hands palms up. After a moment of silence Caleb spoke to the Timeless-One and said,

> "Oh, great and awesome Timeless-One,
> You are before ancient and beyond future,
> Fill us with the fullness of you,
> And fill our minds with Your wisdom and understanding."

Just then a brilliant bright white light came down from heaven like a laser and surrounded them all. The light was humming and pulsing like a heartbeat. Then they heard the voice of the Timeless-One, "Be filled!" Instantly the light shot back up into heaven. For three minutes they all stood still and did not move. As they brought their hands down, Wah'li'si, Saleah and Zoe sang a song,

> "We dance to the beat of Your heart,
> We see by the light of Your glory,
> We hear by the Spirit of Your will,
> And by the fullness of You we sing.
>
> Glory, glory, glory to the Timeless-One
> Holy, holy, holy is the Mighty One
> Glory, glory, glory to the Timeless-One
> We sing, we dance, and we praise You Lord."

When they were finished worshiping the Timeless-One they all stood there for a few seconds and just took in all the Timeless-One had said and done for them. Then with a shout of excitement Christopher said, "Woo-hoo! Yeah! That was awesome!" Then they all laughed.

"What now Caleb?" asked Wah'li'si. "Let's go back to the town square." Caleb replied. "I think the answer lies there." Caleb continued. So, they all headed back to the town square with Wah'ya and Neshoba leading the way.

Land Enchant – Gate of Angelick Village Bryan the Magic Man

Bryan stood at the gate of Angelick Village in relief and said with a sigh, "Finally." The gate to the village had no bars in place; it was just an archway leading into the village. As he started to enter the gate, the voice of Legion came deafeningly loud as an explosion in Bryan's ears growling, "I am here! We are hungry!" Bryan then ran through the gate. As he stood there, just on the other side of the gate, he looked around and saw that the village had been cursed. "The light of the magick is gone." He spoke. Then he thought a minute and said, "The town square." So, he headed for the town square.

Angelick Village

Just as Caleb and the rest reached the town square, Wah'li'si feeling in her spirit stopped and said, "Nasgi asgaya Ahani." Meaning, "He's here." "How do you know?" asked Christopher. "I know." Answered Wah'li'si. Just then the portal appeared again where the statue once stood. It was larger than before and was pulsating very rapidly. Wah'ya moved in front of them, and Neshoba got behind them. The hairs on their necks were standing up as they growled both wolves ready to fight. "Are you guys seeing this?" asked Saleah. As they looked around, they saw the people slowly emerging from within the walls of the buildings, as if the walls were made of molten lava, for the walls turned dark red and began moving like water and heat waves were coming off the buildings. All the people stood about seven feet tall and had angelic wings and they all looked like liquid shadows. Bryan also saw this happening and began to run to the town square.

Bryan ran up to the town square and suddenly stopped when he saw Caleb and the rest. "Who are you!?" he demanded. Caleb stepped forward and said, "We are the ones looking for you." "What!?" answered Bryan.

Then from within the portal came the voice of Legion, growling with a multitude of voices, "Looks like we're all here!" "Caleb!" said Zoe excitedly, "The people . . . things are getting closer!" Just as they all looked around there were about a hundred of these liquid shadow people surrounding the town square. They stood just around the outer edge of the circle of the square. Bryan opened his "Book of Shadows" and found a spell and started to recite it when Legion growled, "I'll take that!" Just then the book flew out of Bryan's hands and disappeared into the portal. "**NO!**" yelled Bryan. Bryan started to go after it; Christopher and Logan grabbed him and Christopher demanded, "No! You can't go in there!" "It's gone, man!" said Logan. "I need my book!" yelled Bryan. "It's gone." explained Logan.

Then from within the portal came the sound of many explosions like the sounds of volcanoes erupting. The winged shadow people fell to their knees and bowed with their faces to the ground and arms stretched out in front of them. "I come, and we are hungry for souls!" growled Legion. Just then the portal turned blood red and started changing shape as if it was trying to grow bigger and couldn't. Then from the portal came Legion, he leaped from within and landed about twenty feet in front of Caleb and the others.

Legion stood about ten feet tall. He stood as a single creature but was made up of what looked like thousands of grotesque little demons. They looked like black and red gooey tar. Individually they moved slowly, but remained in place, forming the one structure of the creature called Legion. Three demons formed Legions mouth, so when he spoke the three demons moved in unison. "So," growled Legion in a multitude of voices, "I have Bryan, the magic man, and Caleb, the high priest of the Timeless-One and his holy regime." Legion took a couple of steps forward, then bent over slightly and growled in a single voice, "We will take all of you to the Stygian Flame, where I will burn you with the blackest of fire and feed on your flesh for all eternity!" Wah'li'si grabbed Saleah and Zoe's hands and said, "Galutsv!" This means, "Come!" "Christopher, Galutsv!" Wah'li'si demanded.

Wah'li'si, Saleah, Zoe and Christopher gathered in a circle and heart-linked with the Timeless-One. Caleb and Logan moved in front of Bryan. "Stay behind us!" demanded Caleb to Bryan. "Heart-linking with the Timeless-One? Huh!" sneered Legion. "I'm not with them!" yelled Bryan as he pushed through Caleb and Logan. "I command you, leave now!" Bryan demanded. Legion raised his left hand and growled, "I am the master, and you are the servant, silence!" At that Bryans lips were fused together. He fell on the ground holding his mouth, moaning. Just then a bright white light came down from heaven and surrounded Wah'li'si, Saleah, Zoe and Christopher. Logan lifted his hands, palms up to heart-link with the Timeless-One as Caleb stepped forward and demanded, "Legion! Legion, you are of old this is true, and in torment you will live forever! Leave this dimension now and go back to your black flame!" "Not without the magic man!" growled Legion. Just then two demons leaped from Legions legs and ran over and grabbed the legs of Bryan. They began pulling Bryan toward Legion. Bryan struggled, trying to kick the demons off. He dug his fingers in the ground trying not to be dragged as his fingernails filled with rocks and dirt, moving along the ground.

The light that surrounded Wah'li'si, Saleah, Zoe and Christopher started crackling like electricity shooting out bolts of lightning. When this happened the winged shadow people stood to their feet and started moving in slowly, toward Caleb and the rest. Caleb lifted his right hand high above his head and said,

"Oh, Timeless-One, You are the God that transcends dimensions,
And makes time the temporal illusion.
Show now, this ancient tormentor,
Your love for all human beings,
And Your hate for all evil."

When Caleb finished speaking, he raised his left hand toward the demons dragging Bryan along the ground when white balls of fire shot out of his hands and struck the demons. The demons exploded with a shriek. Waya and Neshoba ran over and stood by Bryan, guarding him. When the demons exploded Legion growled out in pain, "Ahhh!" Then he demanded, "Attack!" Just then the winged liquid shadow people started moving towards them very rapidly. Caleb whipped his head around and yelled, "Wah'li'si!" as he did, a beam of pure white light shot out from Caleb's hand. Just before the light reached Wah'li'si, Saleah, Zoe and Christopher, Wah'li'si shouted, "NAQUU!" meaning, "Now!" They all quickly turned facing outward from their circle, toward the winged people. At that instant Wah'li'si, Saleah, Zoe and Christopher thrust their hands forward just as the beam of light hit them. The light shot out from their hands and struck the winged people. When the beams hit the people, it paralyzed them instantly and their wings disintegrated and what looked like some kind of liquid covering fell from them. They were normal people under all the disguise and control of Legion. They fell on the ground unconscious.

Legion growled in a multitude of voices saying, "It's not just the magic man I'm taking with me, but all of you, now!" Just then, about a hundred demons jumped off Legion and surrounded the area. The demons became larger as they stood around them waiting for the command. They stood about six feet tall; they were all black and red goo, with razor teeth and nails. The demons stood there breathing heavily. "When you go back through the portal, you are going alone!" demanded Caleb. Without any warning the pure white light of the Timeless-One came down on Caleb and his holy regime. Caleb, then immediately threw a ball of white light at a demon. The demon exploded; Legion growled in pain. Then without letting up Wah'li'si and the others did the same, throwing balls of white light at the demons. Whenever a demon exploded, Legion growled out in anguish and pain. Legion couldn't move because Caleb and the others didn't stop until all the demons were destroyed. Caleb, Wah'li'si and the others moved in such great speed that the demons couldn't get close to them. When the demons were all destroyed, Caleb looked at Legion; He was bent over, laboring to breathe.

Caleb took a few steps toward Legion, thrust his right hand out toward Legion and demanded, "Back to hell!" Just then a pure white light in the shape of a large hand hit Legion in the chest propelling him backward into the portal as he growled with a loud roar. The portal closed with a loud sound like suction.

A mist like silver crystal came in and covered the people that lay unconscious on the ground. After a few seconds it lifted, the people stood to their feet wearing white robes. They had no memory of what happened to them. Bryan stood to his feet and said, "Who are you?" He reached up and touched his lips realizing they were back to normal. Caleb stepped forward and explained, "We are from High Rock." Caleb took three more steps toward Bryan and said, "The Timeless-One sent us to you." Looking around at all the people who were moving in closer to see what was happening, he continued, "He sent us to **all** of you!" Looking back at Bryan Caleb said, "The Timeless-One loves you Bryan, and He wants you to know true power, true joy and true love." "The Timeless-One knows me? He loves me?" asked Bryan as he fell to his knees and wept. Caleb reached over and put his hands on Bryan's shoulders. As he did the people got down on their knees. Then Caleb led them all in a prayer to the Timeless-One. When they were through, they all stood to their feet and shouted for joy. Then Wah'li'si, Saleah and Zoe sang a song and danced.

Song: Great Wonderment

Great God (Great God)
Great Power (Great Power)
Great Love (Great Love)
Great Wonderment (Great Wonderment)
(Repeat)

> You are God, we adore You.
> You are Love, our hands are lifted high.
> You're a Wonderment, and You amaze.
> You are perfect joy, You satisfy.
> (Back to top)

Caleb and the rest stayed in the village for three weeks ministering and teaching about the Timeless-One. At the end of three weeks Caleb and the rest met in the town square. The towns' people followed.

Then out of the sky came the chariot drawn by horses of blue flames. When it landed Christopher said, "Here we go again." Zoe questioned, "Really?" "After all that happened, you're scared of this?" asked Saleah. Zoe teased saying, "Christopher's scared. Christopher's scared." "I'm not scared." Christopher explained. "I'm just a little concerned." "He's scared." Saleah and Zoe said in unison. "Do you want me to hold your hand?" asked Logan. "Funny." Christopher answered. Everyone got into the chariot except Caleb. Caleb walked over to Bryan and handed him a copy of the "Holy Verses" and said, "This is **real** power, and this is **real** magic. With it you can transform hearts, and with it you can overcome evil." Caleb continued, "But, only with a clean heart, a pure mind and a spirit on fire by the Timeless-One." Bryan wept and said, "Thank you, Caleb. Thank you all. You have given us all a great gift." Caleb replied, "Let not the fire go out, my friend." Caleb got into the chariot, and it took off.

It only took about thirty seconds, and they were back at High Rock. The people of High Rock came to meet them, to hear of their adventure. Some stood and some sat on the ground as Caleb and his holy regime told the story of the magic man and the power of the Timeless-One.

15

AS THE DANCERS DANCE

Psalms 149:3

Let them praise His name with the dance; Let them sing praises to Him with the timbrel and harp. (NKJV)

(A scene in hell)

With the sound of volcanic eruptions every thirty seconds mixed with the sounds of millions of people screaming, shouting and moaning in anguish and pain. And the stench of rotting and burning souls mingled with the smell of unholy fervent heat the littlest of gods sits on his throne in deep thought. Then suddenly, with a loud roar he yells for one of his servants, "Corruption!!" Within seconds a hideous looking little demon appears before the littlest of gods, kneeling in fear saying, "Yes, lord Dragon? You, called?" The littlest of gods took in a deep breath and slowly exhaled, much smoke and a low rumble came from his nostrils. "What is the status on Caleb, the High Priest?" he growled. Corruption stood to his feet and turned his head and yelled nervously, "Bring in Caleb's file!" Seconds later a blood dripping demon approached Corruption with a large black book.

Corruption took the book from the demon and walked nervously to the littlest of gods, bowing his head in fear he handed the book to him saying, "Here it is, my lord."

The littlest of gods took the book and held it in his lap. He looked at it intently, rubbing the cover with his hands. The book was very large, and the cover was very firm and black, made of unknown material with raised letters that read, "Caleb, The Enemy of Mine." When he opened it and began to read, the letters started running and dripping off the page like fresh blood from a wound. The littlest of gods began to breathe heavily, and he gripped the book very tightly as his body shook, "What's this?!" He growled. Just then words appeared on the page, as if someone was writing with a pen, it read, "One cannot be killed, when one is already dead. And, since he is dead, he shall never die, says the Lord of Caleb, My friend." The littlest of gods closed the book with a slam and threw to the floor almost hitting Corruption. When it hit the floor, it exploded into a fine dust that covered the entire area of the throne room. The littlest of gods stood to his feet and thrust his fist above his head and yelled at the top of his lungs, "I hate you! I HATE YOU! And I despise . . . Caleb!" His voice echoed throughout hell. He stopped for a second and thought. He sat back down on his throne and an evil smile came on his face as he said, "I've got an idea." Laughing he said again, "I've, got an idea!" Then he stood to his feet again and yelled, "I want Mr. Doubt, the Accuser and the Man of Deception in front of me, NOW!" As he sat back down, he said in a low whisper to himself as he laughed with an evil growl, "These guys are going dancing Ha, ha-ha, ha." He twirled his finger above his head and in a mocking sophisticated voice he said, "Shall we go to the Ball Ha, ha-ha, ha?!" His laughter echoed throughout infernal hell.

(At High Rock)

Wah'li'si walked in the garden just outside High Rock with her two-star pupils, Saleah and Zoe, (Saleah 19 and Zoe 18 years old are cousins and best friends). As they walked, Wah'li'si turned to the girls and said, "The

Timeless-One is Mighty indeed, All Powerful and All Knowing. He is the Song we sing;

He is the Dance we dance and the Spirit in every breath we breathe." "Wah'li'si," said Saleah, "When I dance for the Timeless-One," Saleah lifted her hands up and gracefully twirled around and said, "I feel like I am right in front of Him, in His Throne Room, just the two of us. Oh . . .," she then smiled big as she always does and said, "It is so wonderful." "Yes, it is the same for me." Added Zoe excitedly, "When I sing, it is as though He is reaching out with His hands, grabbing my words and putting them in His heart. I feel He alone hears me; He alone is my audience." "Well said girls, well said." Replied Wah'li'si. At that moment the ground under their feet began to move in a circular motion. Zoe yelled, "Wah'li'si! I can't move my feet!" "What's happening?" screamed Saleah. The air turned green and purple as it violently swirled around them like a whirlwind.

Caleb had just entered the garden and saw this happen. He ran toward Wah'li'si and the girls as fast as he could. Before he could reach them, from within the whirlwind came an evil voice saying, "Come one, come all. It's time for fun. It's time to **FALL Ha, ha-ha ha!**" Wah'li'si grabbed the girl's hands and said, "Hang on!" Just then the ground opened, and they fell through the earth. Right as Caleb reached the area, they were gone. At that instant the whirlwind had stopped, the air returned to normal, and the ground was solid again. Caleb fell to his knees, moving his hands along the ground where they were pulled under calling out, "Wah'li'si, Wah'li'si!" There was no reply. Just then Caleb heard the Voice of the Timeless-One saying, "Fear not Caleb, My friend. Wah'li'si, Saleah and Zoe are in My grip. I AM in control." Caleb stayed on his knees and lifted his hands to the Timeless-One but, said nothing.

"Go back to High Rock, to the Temple and wait." said the Timeless-One, "I will meet you there." Caleb replied saying,

"You, oh Lord, You are in control. We, oh Lord, we are in Your grip.

Blessed be the Timeless-One, Blessed be my God."

Caleb got up and looked at the ground once more. Then looked up at the sky and said, "You are everywhere. You are here and . . ." Caleb looked back at the ground, "You are there." Then he headed back to High Rock.

(The Land of Fraud)

Wah'li'si, Saleah and Zoe stood to their feet and adjusted their eyes to the darkened surroundings they were now in. "Is everyone alright?" asked Wah'li'si. Saleah and Zoe both said, "Yes, we're good." as they brushed themselves off. "Where are we?" asked Zoe. "I don't know, Zoe." Answered Wah'li'si as they all looked around. What they saw was so unreal to them, stalagmites and boulders everywhere, and stalactites hanging in midair. There was no grass or trees, the ground looked like black volcanic rock. Above the stalactites swirled a green and purple liquid and off on the horizon was a dark red glow like something very large was on fire. The only sound that was heard was like a humming that came from the swirling green and purple sky.

Then they heard a voice that said, "Welcome guests, and welcome friends. This is the time for games; this is the time for wits." As they looked around to see where the voice came from Saleah said demanding, "Who are you? Show yourself!" "I am here, I am there. I am in your head, I am . . . everywhere." The voice replied. Then, Wah'li'si and the girls heard a dull tapping sound behind them. When they turned around, they saw a man standing next to a large boulder, tapping it with a cane that he held in his hand. The man was tall, slim and was wearing a black top hat and tails. He had shoulder length straight black hair and a goatee.

"Who are you?" demanded Wah'li'si. "Who am I, who are you? What really matters is . . ." pointing his cane at Wah'li'si and continued, "what you do." Replied the man. The handle of his cane was a head of a goat, with eyes that glowed red. "I know who you are." Said Wah'li'si. "You are the Man of

Deception." "What?" questioned Zoe in unbelief. "I thought he was dead." added Saleah. "What, what, what did you say?" asked the Man of Deception as he swaggered over and stood in front of Wah'li'si. He got inches from her face and looking into her eyes said arrogantly, "What did you say? Do you not think if you try to kill evil, you won't have hell to pay? Hmm, hmm?"

The Man of Deception took a step back and said, "Now!" He turned around quickly and twirled his cane like a baton saying, "Without further ado, we have some special guests," he stopped and turned around, he pointed his cane at all of them and said, "just . . . for . . . you." Saleah and Zoe moved closer to Wah'li'si. "To my right," shouted the Man of Deception like a Big Top announcer. "Coming all the way from . . .. your mind. This man makes you wonder why, question God and makes you cry. Let's hear it for Mr. Doubt!" Applause and shouting echoed loudly, but there were no one around. A spotlight shown on a boulder, then a man appeared out of nowhere standing on top. He was dressed in a black and gray pin-striped suit. He was slim and bald, wearing dark sunglasses. Bowing and waving his hand he smiled and said, "Thank you, thank you." "Isn't he great? Isn't he grand? He's one in a million." Said the Man of Deception as he pointed his cane at Mr. Doubt and continued, "Hey, you're the man." The Man of Deception turned toward Wah'li'si and the girls and said, "Now, we have a real treat. Now, we have a real celebrity. Now, put your hands together. This is now reality!" Another loud applause erupted with no one around as the Man of Deception continued, "Here is the, or your Accuser." Just then a voice came from above them out of the green and purple liquid shouting, "Yes! That's right! I have arrived!" As Wah'li'si, Saleah and Zoe looked up, they saw a man emerging and descending from out of the liquid that floated above them. When the man reached the ground, he stood next to the Man of Deception.

He looked like a middle-aged man with slightly gray, short hair and wearing a red three-piece suit with a black tie. The Man of Deception leaned over to the Accuser and asked, "What do you think?" The Accuser leaned over to the Man of Deception as if to whisper and pointed at Wah'li'si, Saleah and Zoe and demanded saying, "Guilty! Guilty! Guilty!" Then he and the Man of Deception and Mr. Doubt laughed. Their laughter echoed throughout the Land of Fraud.

"Yeliquu! Enough!" demanded Wah'li'si in her native tongue and English. "What is it that you want from us?" she continued. The Man of Deception walked up to Wah'li'si leaned forward and said, "Want from you? Want from the One! Want only one. Want the . . . favorite one." "What?!" demanded Zoe. The Accuser walked around and came up behind Wah'li'si, Saleah and Zoe and said arrogantly, "Caleb! We came for Caleb. And, when we kill him, it will be your fault." "Caleb's not here!" shouted Saleah. "Oh, he's coming. He is coming." assured the Accuser. "Oh, he won't come for these three. Not Caleb, no." said Mr. Doubt. The Man of Deception laughed.

(At High Rock)

When Caleb reached High Rock he went straight to the Temple yard, where Christopher, Logan and Eli'Zur were there waiting for him. "Caleb? What's wrong?" "We're not all here yet." Caleb answered. Just then walking up to them was Bryan from Angelick Village. "Where did you come from?" Christopher asked. "How did you get here?" asked Logan. "I was in Angelick Village studying the Holy Verses when the Word appeared before me. He said that I must come and help Caleb. In that instant I was standing in High Rock." "Awesome!" said Christopher. "What's going on Caleb?" asked Bryan. "Let's wait on the Timeless-One." Replied Caleb. Then all raised their hands, palms up and heart-linked with the Timeless-One.

After a few minutes the Word stood amid them and said, "Peace is multiplied in you all". The men never brought their hands down, and never opened their eyes. Then the Word said to them, "The littlest of gods has sent three of his chief principalities to kill you, Caleb. They have taken Wah'li'si,

Saleah and Zoe to the Land of Fraud. I will send you there. You will defeat the principalities and return with Wah'li'si, Saleah and Zoe."

Land of Fraud

Caleb brought his hands down and opened his eyes. He and the others now stood in the Land of Fraud. "Hey .... guys." He spoke. Then Christopher and the rest brought their hands down and saw where they were. "Land of Fraud, I guess?" asked Christopher sarcastically. "I've been here before." Declared Caleb. "This is where I killed the Man of Deception." He continued. "What now, Caleb?" asked Eli'Zur. Just then a little white light appeared in the green and purple canopy above their heads. The light started moving away from them. "We need to follow it." said Caleb. "I agree." said Eli'Zur. The others said the same.

In another part of the Land of Fraud the Man of Deception said, "Oh, my. Oh, me. You just won't believe. We have company." "Caleb!" whispered Wah'li'si. Mr. Doubt walked up behind Wah'li'si and said, "You know he can't win. He's going to die!" The Accuser got in her face and said, "And it's your entire fault. You shouldn't have taken the girls outside High Rock. They are all going to die because of you!" Wah'li'si put her hands over her face and sobbed, "I'm sorry girls. I'm sorry I got you in to this!" "Don't listen to them!" demanded Saleah. "They're lying Wah'li'si!" yelled Zoe. "Caleb is coming, and the Timeless-One is with him!" Wah'li'si brought her hands down and shook her head and glared at the Accuser and demanded in her native language, **"Agisdiyi Oniditlv Ayv Tsvsgina!"** which means, **"Get behind me devil!"**

The Accuser turned his head away from Wah'li'si and went, "Hmm!" and walked away. The Man of Deception swaggered over to Wah'li'si and the girls and said, "We are strong? We have no fear. Soon we will see. Soon, all will bleed!" Just then chains shot up out of the ground and clasped around the wrists of Wah'li'si, Saleah and Zoe. "Wah'li'si!?" shouted Zoe. Saleah pulled at the chains and demanded, "What do you think you're doing!?" Wah'li'si jerked the chains and said sternly, "**Nihi Uha Gotlvnvhi A Equa Galidastanv!**" which means, "You have made a big mistake!" The Man of Deception twirled his cane walked around them and said, "Do you feel? Do you hear? Ah, yes! I smell fear!" At that instant an evil grotesque looking creature crawled out from the solid ground. It was about four feet tall and walked on four legs, although the two front legs looked more like extra-long arms. It had no hair and black in color. There were holes where eyes should be, but it acted as though it could see. Acid-like saliva dripped from its over-sized mouth with razor looking teeth. It breathed heavily with smoke shooting out from its nostrils. It walked over to Wah'li'si and the girls moving its head from side to side. It began circling them very slowly. "Don't move girls." Said Wah'li'si. "Do you like my pet?" asked The Man of Deception. "I call him Fred." "Soon I'll call him dead!" shouted Zoe as she jerked on the chains. "Judgment has come to these three, yes!" said The Accuser as he stretched his hands out towards Wah'li'si and the girls. Just then green looking lightning came forth from his fingertips and went towards the girls. It stopped in front of them and encircled them and the demon creature, making a glowing green cage. Mr. Doubt walked up to the cage and said in a mocking tone, "There's no hope, no hope, no hope." "Don't listen to them! The Timeless-One is here! They're the ones with no hope!" Assured Wah'li'si. Then Wah'li'si spoke to the Timeless-One,

> "Blessed art thou Oh Lord, All Holy and True,
> You never leave us, and You never forsake,
> Wherever we go, You are there,
> If we go to the highest high, You are there,
> If we descend into the depths of the earth, You are there.
> Vdadilvquotanv, Galvquodiyu Ale Udohiyu . . . Nasgi winigalisda.
> (Blessed, Holy and True . . . Amen.)

Caleb and the men pressed on. Then, Christopher broke the silence, he said, "You know, there is a whole lot of nothing here." "I've been here before." replied Bryan. "You've been here?" asked Logan. "Yes," answered Bryan. "During many of my vision quests." Bryan continued, "Just beneath us is the dimension of the Stygian Flame. That's where Legion came from." "No way!" said Christopher. "All is well. The Timeless-One is with us." Encouraged Caleb. Just then they heard the voice of the Man of Deception, "Welcome, welcome, welcome to the greatest show . . . uh . . . somewhere other than earth" As they looked, walking toward them was the Man of Deception, Mr. Doubt and the Accuser. "Where is Wah'li'si, Saleah and Zoe!" demanded Caleb. "Where, who, how, what are they? Hmm, that is a mystery." Eli'Zur drew his spirit sword and rushed at them. Before he reached the three the Accuser threw his hands out in front of him, and the ground gave way in front of Eli'Zur opening into great chasm. Eli'Zur almost fell in. Looking down into it about three hundred feet down, he saw a river of rushing lava. In the lava was what looked like people, they were being pulled along by the current as they cried out in pain. Caleb and the rest ran up to Eli'Zur and looked down into the rushing river of fire. As they looked, they could see demonic creatures climbing up the chasm wall. There were hundreds of them. "It's Time for us to go; time for you to die. Watch that first step, it is a fright." Said the Man of Deception as the three vanished. When they vanished, the men could hear the laughter of a multitude of people.

> Caleb stepped back and drew his Spirit Sword and shouted,
> "Strengthen Your soldiers. Empower Your mighty men!
> Fill us with Your righteous anger, and let Your fury rise up in us!
> Give us the rage of the Lion and the swiftness of the leopard!
> Oh Timeless-One Your Power never fails!"

Just then the others drew their swords and, a bright pure white light came down on them. As the light covered the men, the Word stood among them.

The men became frozen, so they were unable to move a muscle. The Word walked around the men touching each of them on their heads and saying, "Valiant men you are, courageous and strong. I give you all a double portion of my fury and fierce hatred for evil. I now make you a whirlwind of fury and a storm of violent warriors! Wield your Spirit Swords and fight, for you have already conquered, you have already prevailed!" At that, the light and the Word was gone. The men stood there and looked at each other for a second. "I feel as though a have electricity running through my body." said Logan. "The Timeless-One has empowered us." Caleb explained. "Let's do this!" Eli'Zur said with authority in his voice.

They turned around and saw the demons crawling up, out of the chasm. They were all about four feet tall and black as coal. They all looked like the creature that is caged up with Wah'li'si and the girls. When they weren't growling, the only word they hissed was, "Die!" The men stood back-to-back making a circle, swords out in front. The beasts surrounded them, as they bounced up and down like if they had springs in their legs. All the while they kept striking at the air towards the men. "What are they waiting for!?" demanded Christopher. "Come on!!" he shouted at the demons. At that Christopher ran toward the demons, he did a flip in the air, his hands never touched the ground. He landed on his feet just inches from a demon. "Wow!" he said amazed. Then he wielded his sword and cut off the demon's head with one motion. Then Caleb and the others charged the beasts with great speed. They moved like master swordsmen. They were swifter than the tiger and their strikes were faster than the scorpion. As each sword penetrated the demons, the demon would burst into flame and vanish. Caleb and the men killed more than two hundred demons in a matter of minutes. Bryan had the last demon at the edge of the chasm with his sword at the demon's head, he said, "Tell Legion I'm back! And the Power of the Timeless-One is with me!" Then he did a spinning back kick to the demon's head.

The demon went flying backwards into the chasm, into the rushing river of fire. "That was awesome!" shouted Christopher. "The Timeless-One has given us a great gift." Caleb said. "Now, let us use it to free Wah'li'si, Saleah and Zoe." "Let's do it!" Logan said excitedly. "One thing though," added Christopher. "How do we get across the big hole in the ground?" Then they all turned and looked at the chasm.

The sound of a mighty rushing wind came, but the men felt nothing on their faces. As they all looked around Caleb said, "Do not say a word. Listen." Then, within the sound of the mighty wind, very faint, very soft, they could hear the Voice of the Word saying, "Walk. Walk, walk. I AM your bridge of Salvation. Walk." So, Caleb walked to the edge of the chasm, looked straight ahead and said,

> "Into Your hands, I step.
> Into Your grace, I fly.
> In Your Power, I trust.
> In Your Love, I cling."

Then he started walking across the chasm in midair. It was about a hundred feet to the other side. When Caleb got across, he turned and said, "Come." Christopher said, "No way, man. No way!" He went to the edge of the chasm and knelt down; he reached his hand down to feel where Caleb stepped out. There was nothing there. Eli'Zur walked over and said to Christopher, "Step aside." Then he walked across. Before he reached the other side, Christopher reached down and felt nothing. There was nothing solid they are walking on. Then Bryan was next, and then Logan. Now it was Christopher's turn. "Come on, man!" shouted Logan. "I can't!" yelled Christopher. "Let's heart-link." said Caleb. So, Caleb and the men heart-linked with the Timeless-One on one side of the chasm, and Christopher stood at the edge, looking down into the chasm on the other side. As the men heart-linked a bridge started appearing across the chasm.

It began on the side Caleb and the men were on and slowly extended to Christopher's side. Christopher watched as it came near him. The bridge was transparent red, blood red, and it was smooth as glass. Then, Christopher heard the Voice of the Timeless-One, He said, "Now, you see. Now, believe!" "I do see. And I do believe." Christopher responded as he stepped on to the bridge and walked across. When Christopher stepped off the bridge, he walked over to Caleb and said, "I believe man. I really, believe." Caleb put his hand on Christopher's shoulder and said, "Good, very good." Logan walked over to Caleb and Christopher and put his hands on each of their shoulders, leaned in and said, "Now, let's go kick some demon butt!" So, they headed in the direction the Man of Deception went.

Before the Man of Deception, the Accuser and Mr. Doubt arrived back where Wah'li'si and the girls were caged, Wah'li'si said to Saleah and Zoe, "Let's sing a song, shall we?" "A song?" questioned Zoe. "Yes." Responded Wah'li'si, "There is much power in praise and worship." "Let's do it." said Saleah. So, Wah'li'si led the girls in a song of praise and deliverance.

"Oh, Holy One, You stretched out the heavens and hung the stars in place,
And in much excitement, You made the earth with the sound of Your Voice,
The angels gasped as You formed man with Your very own hands,
And with great joy breathed the breath of life into him, and now we live.

Oh, we worship You, Oh we worship you,
Creator of heaven, Creator of earth,
Creator of spirits, Creator of life
We sing our song, we dance our dance,
We praise You for, our deliverance."

As they sang, the chains fell from them to the floor, then they began to dance. As they did the demon that was caged with them vanished and the cage disappeared. Yet, they did not stop singing and dancing.

As the Man of Deception, the Accuser and Mr. Doubt got closer to where Wah'li'si and the girls were, they could hear the singing, only it sounded like a great multitude of singers, singing praise.

A bright light came down and covered Wah'li'si and the girls as they danced and sang in the Spirit. Just then, the Man of Deception, the Accuser and Mr. Doubt could see them as they approached. Surrounding the three women were fifty angelic warriors, with swords drawn. "What is this, what is this?" said the Man of Deception. "This is my domain! This is my world!" Then, from behind them came Caleb and his Holy Regime. "Man of Deception!" yelled Caleb. "So much for a surprise attack." said Christopher. The Man of Deception turned around to see Caleb and his men just a few feet away.

"Oh, my." said the Man of Deception. "It is he, it is me. The beast and the king." As he motioned to himself as the king. "The king of losers." replied Christopher. "Let Wah'li'si and the girls go!" demanded Caleb. "As you can see Priest, they are not caged. They are free to go, I've got what I was sent for." replied the Man of Deception. "What were you sent for?" asked Bryan. "Bryan, is it you? Yes, it's you!" the Man of Deception asked as he walked closer to Bryan and brought his sunglasses down to the end of his nose and looked over the top of them. "It's been a long time. Yes, it has. Hmm?" I, we were sent for the Priest. But now this is a treat. A Priest, a traitor and three sycophants." "Psycho-what?" asked Christopher. "What did he say?" demanded Christopher.

"So," the Man of deception said as he turned and walked back to the Accuser and Mr. Doubt. He stopped and turned quickly to face Caleb and the men.

Opening wide his arms and slightly bowing he said, "Shall we begin?" Christopher, Logan and Eli'Zur quickly drew their swords. Caleb reached his hand out motioning them to put them back and said, "That's not what he is talking about." "Oh, you remember, you remember." The Man of Deception said with an evil grin.

Music filled the Land of Fraud as Wah'li'si, Saleah and Zoe continued dancing and worshiping as the mighty angels stood watch. They did not know what was happening just a few feet away with the Man of Deception and Caleb.

The Man of Deception twirled his cane around his neck, then slammed it on the ground in front of him and said, "Let the games begin, let the festivities commence!" Then, the Man of Deception walked closer toward Caleb and his men and said, "So, Priest, where is your Father? Where is your God? Where, is your Christ? He left you here to wonder, He left you here to ponder, He left you here to die!" Mr. Doubt and the Accuser applauded and said, "Very good. Well done."

Caleb walked over to the Man of Deception and looked him square in the eyes and said, "The littlest of gods is a god of wonders." "Caleb!" demanded Christopher. "He wonders how, he wonders when and wonders why. And wonders where." Continued Caleb.

Wah'li'si, Saleah and Zoe never stopped dancing and singing. The mighty angels stood all around them with swords drawn. Demons crawled up from the solid ground and moved toward Wah'li'si and the girls and surrounded them. The Angels never moved from their position.

Caleb demanded the man of deception, saying, "We are not doing this, this time! We're taking the women and leaving this place!" Then he drew his sword with much force. His men did the same. "Send your demons back from where they came! And you go with them!" Demanded Caleb.

The man of deception, the Accuser and Mr. Doubt raised their left hand up outstretched in front of them toward Caleb and his men. When they did, what looked like green lightning shot out from their hands toward Caleb. Caleb immediately with one swift motion deflected the lightning with his sword. The lightning bounced back and hit the man of deception, the Accuser and Mr. Doubt. The three exploded into a fine black dust.

The demons that had surrounded the women and the angels turned on Caleb and his men. Caleb and his men were ready for a battle, but before the demons could get close, the angels that were protecting the women turned and shot arrows into the demons. As the arrows penetrated the demons, the demons exploded with a shriek.

The angels vanished, all that remained was the dancers and Caleb and his men.

Caleb and Wah'li'si hugged, when they finished hugging when they let go, they were all back at High Rock. The people of High Rock gathered around as Caleb told the of what happened as the dancers danced.

The End.

16

BEFORE ANCIENT PSALMUS 2

Caleb and his mentor, the wise and aged one, the Psalmus sat in front of peaceful campfire. They sat there quietly for a long time when the Psalmus spoke saying,

Psalmus: "In the beginning God created the heavens and the earth,

The earth was formless and void, and darkness was over the surface of the deep, and the Spirit of God was moving over the surface of the waters." (Genesis 1:1,2 NASB)

Caleb: "Tell me again teacher, how did it happen? How did Gods perfect creation become formless and void? How, did it become desolate and dark?"

Psalmus: "It all started in ancient times, before time began, with one angel. One cherub, who was a living creature before the throne of Elohim, the Timeless-One. He was beautiful, blameless and covered with every precious stone in heaven. He was on the Holy Mountain of God and walked in the midst the stones of fire. Then pride entered him, and violence and darkness followed. He wanted to be like the Most High.

The Timeless-One's perfect creation; all the heavens and the earth became a battle ground between the Dragon Lucifer who later would become known as the littlest of gods and his fallen angels, and Michael and his holy warriors. The universe was on fire."

Caleb: One of the Timeless-One's creation wanted to be God? Amazing.

Psalmus: "Now, this is how I heard it, from my teacher and his teacher before him and his teacher before him. Before time existed Lucifer the cherub that covers, the light bearer and worship leader in heaven was walking in the midst of the stones of fire when he approached the crystal sea of glass that is before the throne of Elohim the Most High the Timeless-One. He stopped and gazed intently at his reflection in the sea of glass. He saw his beauty, his perfection and his power. At that instant pride could visibly be seen entering him. Immediately his countenance changed. His heart turned black with hate, and thoughts of envy and rebellion set in. Lucifer said to himself."

> "I will ascend to heaven;" said Lucifer, "I will raise my throne above the stars of God! And I will sit on the mount off assembly in the recesses of the north! I will ascend above the heights of the clouds; I will make myself like the Most High! I will be God!

> Listen to my words.
> All ye host of heaven
> Listen to my words.
> I will show you the way.

> Hear my wondrous symphony.
> My words are sweet as honey.
> Hear now sons of God.
> And all power I will give to thee.

Listen to my words.
Wisdom is your reward.
Listen to my words.
And we will take the throne.

For I will be like God
Follow me!
For I am God
Follow me!"

Caleb: He's insane.

Psalmus: "Lucifer, now called the Dragon went out deceiving and recruiting angels, as well as earth dwellers, into his rebellion against Elohim.

These earth dwellers inhabited an earth we do not know. The earth we live on is not the earth that existed before time. This earth is where the Dragon had his throne and where the deception grew.

It didn't take long before all the earth dwellers and a third of the angels followed the Dragon, Lucifer into a revolt against Elohim, the Timeless-One. The earth dwellers built a temple and set up altars to the Dragon and began to worship the creature instead of the creator. They sacrificed their young upon the altar of the Dragon and engaged in immoral sexual acts of worship.

The angels that followed the Dragon in the revolt set up camp on a nearby planet that we call Mars. There they planned their next move against The Timeless-One and built monuments to the Dragon.

God called for His Archangel Michael, and as He waited for Michael, The Timeless One sat on His throne and spoke these words.

Why do the nations rage?
Why do they plot against me?
Why do they turn away from me?
Why do they hate me . . . Why?

If they return to me
Then I will save them
If they repent
Then I will heal them

Seek me
I am right here.
Cry out to me.
I will hear.
(Back to 1st verse)

The kings of the earth
The Dragon of the air
They have come together.
Against the Lord and His Anointed One

Let Us break their bands apart.
And scatter them to the wind.
Let them run away like blind pigs.
As He who sits on the throne laugh

You imagine in vain.
And fantasize on empty schemes.
Your anger is full of hate.
NOW, taste the wrath of my fury!

Caleb: The Timeless-One was very angry.

Psalmus: "Elohim spoke to Michael saying, 'Lucifer has betrayed us. He has turned many of your brothers as well as the earth dwellers against us. Now, gather your brothers, my sons, who have remained, for now I give to you a new word . . . **WAR!** War has come to my kingdom from within my kingdom. War never was, and now is and will be. Lucifer is no longer to be known as Lucifer the light bearer but, he shall be forever called Satan, the enemy of God. The Dragon of old.'"

Psalmus: "The earth dwellers made for themselves weapons of brass and steel. And built fortresses and traps. Most of the Dragons army was on Mars preparing for battle. The dragon set up for himself a temple and a throne on Mars and called for all the earth dwellers to worship him and Mars as their Gods. That is why it is called Mars today, for he is the one who makes war.

"Michael and his holy warriors positioned themselves between Mars and the Earth. As they waited, they worshiped Elohim saying,

**Holy, holy, holy
Is the Lord of eternity.
Holy, holy, holy
You are the All in All**

**Glory to God in the highest
Jealous is Your Name
Creator of all that is.
Adonai Shaddai, You forever reign**

**Holy, holy, holy
You are before ancient.
Holy, holy, holy
You inhabit Eternity.**

Caleb: Beautiful.

Psalmus: "Without warning the Dragon tilted his head back, opened his mouth and spewed out lava-like fire towards the sky, aimed at Michael. Michael could see the fire coming from the planet; it looked like a monstrous fiery serpent coming right at him. Michael lifted his shield just before the fiery serpent hit him. The serpent smashed into the shield and bounced off, then crashed into the earth causing the entire earth to violently shake to and fro like a drunkard. Oceans poured out onto the land and swept over the cities like someone emptied a cup of water on a tiny anthill. Mountains crumbled like sandcastles and land masses split apart. A third of all earth dwellers perished as well as a third of all the animals.

"Michael with a thousand of his warriors lifted their swords and pointed them at the planet mars, the point where the fiery serpent came from. With loud popping sounds, balls of fire shot out from the tips of the swords and hit the Dragons temple and the surrounding area, exploding on impact leaving behind great craters. The Dragon's temple was completely destroyed. Then Michael and his warriors lifted their swords and fired on the planet once more. Before the balls of fire reached the planet, the Dragon and his fallen ones leaped from the surface of mars.

Psalmus: "The Dragon divided his army into thirds. A third he sent to nearby planets as a diversion.

A third headed straight for Michael and his warriors. This was done so the Dragon could take the rest with him to the earth to command from his temple there.

"Michael divided his warriors as well. A third went after the Dragons army that went to the nearby planets, and a third stayed and fought the ones that came straight at them. Michael took the rest and went after the Dragon.

"The fighting was fierce. The Universe was on fire. The planets that were once lush and beautiful were being destroyed by the angelic exploding fire balls and the chain whips of lightning. All the rainbows and crystals that lighted the heavens were being destroyed.

"Before that great and terrible war in the Heavenlies there was no darkness, no night... No black space, only light. The universe was full of multi-colored rainbows of purple, green, red and yellow, and hundreds of other colors. There were seas of diamonds and gems and stones unknown to us today that filled the heavens. Swirls of different colored crystals moved around the earth like a warm transparent canopy. God, the angels and the earth dwellers inhabited the same multi-space dimension. There were no spirit world and physical world, it was all one. Now, all that was changing.

"Elohim created a special place for the Dragons fallen ones; a prison called Tartarus. A place of absolute darkness, darkness that can be felt. It is a place for punishment for the evil that the Dragon and the fallen ones brought upon all creation. Elohim put Tartarus in the thirteenth dimension. No created being was permitted to enter this dimension, for once you were there, there was no leaving. Complete isolation, separation, silence and darkness. Tartarus is the abode of the wicked.

"Michael's warriors were more powerful than the Dragons fallen ones. This is how they overcame the fallen ones; Michael's warriors would fire on them with their swords hitting them with the balls of fire, then another warrior would sling the chain whip of lightning, binding the fallen one around their chest, pinning their arms against the body.

They were then paralyzed. A porthole emerged in space that led to the thirteenth dimension, straight into Tartarus.

The holy warriors then slung the bound fallen ones into the porthole, right into Tartarus. Their abode for all eternity.

"With no effort Michael's warriors gathered the earth dwellers together in one place, a large plane east of Baal City. Elohim named that place, "the First Judgment". Elohim placed Cherubim at the four corners of the plane. A bright thin red light passed between the Cherubim, making a force field around the plane. If any of the earth dwellers tried to go through the force field, they were incinerated. There was no escaping.

"Michael and his warriors approached the temple of the Dragon, there were no fallen ones in sight. Michael had his warriors surround the temple while he and two of his angels went up the stairs to go inside. Just before they reached the door it swung open. It didn't faze Michael or his angels, they kept walking. Once through the door, it slammed shut behind them. And at that instant the fallen ones materialized surrounding Michael's warriors with swords drawn. It was a standoff.

"It was very dark within the temple. The only light inside was glowing green crystals that lined a path right up to the throne, that was about two hundred feet in front of them. Another green light shined down on the throne where the Dragon sat. As Michael and the two warriors walked closer, fallen ones stepped out of the darkness and lined the path, standing by the green crystals. Halfway to the throne Michael called out and said, "**Satan! You traitor!** I have come to take you to stand before **THE THRONE! Before Elohim, your creator!**" "Oh, I don't think so Michael." arrogantly replied the Dragon as he stood to his feet. Michael moved closer and stopped about twenty feet from the throne and demanded, "You know the law! You will be tried and sentenced for treason! Elohim rules!" "Not, anymore." boasted the Dragon as he lifted his hands. When he did, a bright light emanated from him, but faded quickly. He moved his head back and forth looking at his hands. "What is this!?" he demanded.

"The Timeless-One is the source of light, not you!" said Michael. "Now your darkness will shine!" continued Michael,

"You may be able to fool earth dwellers and other angels in your fallen state, but as for those who belong and remain to Elohim your darkness shines bright! Let us go, for judgment has come."

Psalmus: "The Dragon stepped down from the throne and walked over to Michael and said, "Michael, Michael, look, you're my brother. Can't you see, together we can rule the universe?" Michael drew his sword and put the tip of it on the floor with both hands on the handle and said, "You know the Law, and you know Elohim! He says, 'I Am God, We are One. There is **NO** other!'" The Dragon took another step toward Michael and asked, "Indeed, has God said, 'You are sons of God. My perfect creation. Now reign with me.'" Michael answered proclaiming, "We **are** Gods' sons, but we are not God. He is the Creator; we are the creation! Don't ever forget that!"

"The Dragon turned his back to Michael and said, "So, you will not join me." "No," Michael answered, "I will not. I am here to take you back. You will stand before Elohim and answer for your crimes." The Dragon answered slowly, "I don't think so." Just then he quickly turned around and opened his mouth. When he did lava like fire spewed out towards Michael. At that instant all the fallen ones in the temple, outside and in space raised their swords to attack. Michael lifted his sword to block the fire, but when he did the fire had stopped before it reached him. As he looked, the Dragon was frozen as was all the fallen ones. Then Elohim Spoke and all herd his voice, even the ones who were frozen, "**NO MORE!** That is enough. I regret I created any of this." Then He said. "Michael, get them up here!" "Yes, Your Majesty." Michael answered.

"Michael bound the Dragons hands behind his back with a rope of lightning. His warriors did the same to the fallen ones. In a wink of an eye, they were all standing before the Throne in the third heaven. The earth dwellers were left behind on the earth.

"The courtroom was completely full. There were archangels, cherubim, seraphim and living creatures present.

The Timeless-One was seated on the throne. Surrounding the throne was a rainbow of different colored gems that emanated lightnings and thunders. Two cherubim stood in front of the Throne, one on the left and one on the right. They faced each other, and each had six wings full of eyes. With two wings they covered themselves, with two they watched the courtroom, and with two they extended toward each other covering the throne. Two seraphim of fire flew to and fro in front of the Throne singing, **"Holy, holy, holy, is the Lord God Almighty. All is full of His glory."** Archangels lined the entire courtroom. This courtroom was large enough to hold the hundreds of thousands of angels that rebelled. The courtrooms walls were pure white and about fifty feet high with windows that lined the top that had now windows. The doors were just as high as the walls, and they were made out of something that looked like ivory. The floor was made of pure transparent gold. The ceiling was made of blue and purple gemstones that also was transparent. The Word was present, standing at Gods right hand. Also, the Spirit was there, hovering over the Throne."

Just and True
You are worthy to be praised.
Wisdom and Power
You are worthy to be praised.

Holy, holy, holy
Is the Lord God Almighty
Holy, holy, holy
All is full of Your glory.

Righteous and Strength
You are worthy to be praised.
Glory and Honor
You are worthy to be praised.
(chorus)

Psalmus: "The Timeless-One lifted His right hand and every angel fell to their knees, even those who did not want to, went to their knees. Elohim spoke with the sound of thunder, and when he did the whole Throne room shook. He said, "I will deal with the earth dwellers first."

"The crystal canopy collapsed, when it did the crystals rained down on the earth. As the crystals hit the ground, they dissolved into the earth leaving no trace of them. The sky rolled back like a scroll with lightning and thunders. A great wind started blowing. All the earth dwellers looked to the sky as a white light broke through the empty space above them. Then the earth dwellers heard the voice of Elohim thunder saying, "Earth dwellers, hear now My voice! You have betrayed Me. You have turned your back on Me. You have rejected Me. Now, I will turn My back on you! Now, I will reject you!" All the earth dwellers fell to their knees, crying and moaning saying, "We were deceived! We were deceived!" "From this time on," Elohim continued, "you will no longer have bodies. You will be *tohu v'bohu*, formless and void, just as the earth will become. You will know only darkness. You will roam the earth and will find no peace, and no rest. Evil you chose, and evil you will be. This was your first judgment, the second is coming." All the earth dwellers wailed and moaned, pulling at their hair and throwing dust on their heads.

"Then there was a short, loud sound like a pop. The wailing stopped, and there was silence, total silence for about three minutes in heaven and on earth. Then Elohim told one of the angels standing in the courtroom saying, "Take the bowl from the Word and pour it out on the earth. This is My sentence on the earth dwellers." So the angel took the bowl from the Word and poured it out on the earth dwellers.

Within seconds the earth dwellers began screaming and wailing in pain as their bodies melted and dissolved as if acid was poured on them. What was left was formless multi-dimensional malevolent beings that we call, demons.

"Then Elohim called for another angel saying, "Take the bow and the arrow from the Word and fire the arrow into the universe." So the angel walked over and took the bow and the arrow from the Word and fired the arrow out into the universe. As the arrow headed towards earth the universe began to change in all dimensions. Planets melted and became formless. They were just liquid metals and gasses with no shape. Total blackness filled the universe. No rainbows, no crystals to light the universe, just absolute nothingness. The earth also became *tohu v'bohu,* formless and void.

"The Timeless-One thundered, saying to the fallen ones, "You were my sons, full of beauty and full of power. I created you before the universe. I loved you all. Now, you are banished from my sight. You will roam the earth to fro with the formless ones. **BE GONE!**" Just then the floor of the courtroom opened under the fallen ones, and all fell through. They fell to the earth that is now in a black liquid state.

"Now, the only one left for judgment was the Dragon, Satan. He was alone in the middle of the courtroom, kneeling before Elohim. Then The Timeless-One thundered again saying,

"You had the seal of perfection, full of wisdom and perfect in beauty.

You were in Eden, the garden of God; Every precious stone was your covering: The ruby, the topaz and the diamond; The beryl, the onyx and the jasper; The lapis lazuli, the turquoise and the emerald; And the gold. The workmanship of your settings and sockets, was in you. On the day that you were created they were prepared.

You were the anointed cherub who covers, and I placed you there. You were on the holy mountain of God; You walked in the midst of the stones of fire.

You were blameless in your ways, from the day you were created until unrighteousness was found in you.

By the abundance of your trade, you were internally filled with violence, and you sinned; Therefore, I have cast you as profane from

the mountain of God. And I have destroyed you, O covering cherub, from the midst of the stones of fire.

Your heart was lifted up because of your beauty; you corrupted your wisdom by reason of your splendor. I cast you to the ground; I put you before kings, that they may see you.

By the multitude of your iniquities, In the unrighteousness of your trade you profaned your sanctuaries. Therefore, I have brought fire from the midst of you; it has consumed you, and I have turned you to ashes on the earth in the eyes of all who see you." (Ezekiel 28:12-19)

"The Timeless-One motioned with His hand to Michael. Michael took the Dragon by the chains that bound him and stood him to his feet. "Do you have anything to say before you are sentenced?" asked Elohim. "Yes, I do!" demanded the Dragon. The Dragon took two steps forward and looked up at the throne and growled, "This is just the beginning! You can cast me out, but I will ascend to Heaven! I will raise my throne above the stars of God! I will sit enthroned on the mount of assembly, on the utmost heights of the sacred mountain! I will ascend above the tops of the clouds! I will make myself like the Most High! **I, will, be, God**!" Then the floor opened beneath him, and he fell to earth like lightning. The Word walked over to the opening in the floor and watched as Satan fell to earth and said, **"How you have fallen from Heaven, O morning star, son of the dawn. You have been cast down to the earth, you who once laid low the nations. You are brought down to the grave, to the depths of the pit. Those who see you will stare at you, and ponder your fate, saying, 'Is this the man who shook the earth and made kingdoms tremble, the man who made the world a desert and overthrew it's cities?'** "(Isaiah 14:12,15,16,17)

"When the Dragon landed on the black shapeless earth, he stood to his feet. His fallen ones and the demons surrounded him and began circling him saying, "Is this the one!? Ha! You were going to make us gods, now look at you. You, who laid low the nations, ha! You are nothing!" The Dragon looked to the black, empty sky and thrust his fist up and yelled," This is isn't over! This is just the beginning!!!"

"The Word looked down on the earth and said, "You are right, this is, the beginning."

Song: Beyond

**Beyond the recesses of the north
Beyond eternity
Beyond all the stars above
Beyond all our eyes can see**

**You are holy, holy, holy.
You are holy, holy, holy.
You are holy, holy, holy.
Beyond, beyond all**

Caleb: Your insights are great. I will share this at the next Day of Praise.

The End

SONGS AND PRAYERS OF A WARRIOR PRIEST

Praise, worship and prayer are essential in living a Christian life. We cannot battle the powers of evil without them. With prayer and praise, we are communing (heart-linking) with God, and when we are in <u>constant</u> communication with the Timeless-One we receive power through the Holy Spirit to engage in war with the littlest of gods and his unholy army. The attacks of the littlest of gods will then be futile.

With prayer, we come before the Lord with our needs and thanksgivings. Holding up our lost loved ones, those who are sick, and thanking Him for all that He has done in our lives (and all He is going to do).

With praise and worship, we glorify, lift up, and exalt our Lord and King. When we lift Him up, He holds us up. The Psalmus says "Rejoice in the Lord, O you righteous! For praise from the upright is beautiful." (Psalm 33:1 NKJ)

And in return for our praise and prayers, the Lord blesses, energizes and fills us with the Holy Spirit and His Holy Fire, so we can stand against the littlest of gods and his demons and crush them under our feet.

Prayer:

Ephesians 6:18, "With every prayer and petition, pray at all times in the Spirit, and to this end be alert, with all perseverance and requests for all the saints."

1Thessalonians 5:17 says, "Pray without ceasing."

Prayer is talking to God. Many people say, "I don't know how to pray." If you can talk, you can pray, but also you have to listen.

Sometimes if you are just still and quiet you can hear God speaking. Not audibly, but in your spirit, you can hear Him. Not to say He doesn't speak audibly, He can do whatever He wants, but if we just listen, He will speak to us. Prayer is <u>talking and listening</u> to God our Father. He doesn't want to hear some mantra or some rehearsed chant, and it doesn't have to be at any specific time of day. You don't have to kneel, lay or stand in any certain way. Just as you go through the day talk to God your Father, tell Him your concerns or just tell Him you're having a great day.

So, heart-link with The Timeless-One, our Father in Heaven, every day and every night, all the time.

Praise and Worship:

John 4:23 "But the hour is coming, and is now here, when the true worshipers will worship the Father in spirit and truth, for the Father is seeking such people to worship him."

John 4:24 "God is spirit, and those who worship him must worship in spirit and truth."

Psalm 9:2 "I will be glad and exult in you; I will sing praise to your name, O Most High."

Psalm 95:2 "Let us come into his presence with thanksgiving; let us make a joyful noise to him with songs of praise!"

Psalm 150:2 "Praise him for his mighty deeds; praise him according to his excellent greatness!"

When we praise and worship God: 1. we are proclaiming that He is God, that there is no other God that lives, and without Him we would not exist. 2. We are giving Him what He deserves; honor, glory, adoration and applause. 3. We are telling God we love Him; we fear Him and we are in awe of Him.

Worship is a heart thing not a head thing. A person cannot just go through the motions when praising God, because you're not, you are just saying words. God knows the heart of a person. "Worship the Lord in spirit and in truth", the scripture says. So, come before the Lord wherever you are and give our God **applause** for who He is and what He has done, and what He is going to do in your life.

How do we praise and worship? We give thanks, we sing, we dance, we play instruments, we shout, we clap our hands, we lift our hands, we pray, and we fall on our knees and our face before our God.

When do we worship? Anytime and anywhere, that's the best time.

Sing Hallelujah!
Give God a big round of applause!

On the following pages are the songs and prayers of Caleb and his holy regime. I hope they are a blessing to you.

Songs
And
Prayers
From
The Invitation

This is a song of praise from Caleb to God on his way to meet Mr. Wizard.

In this song Caleb acknowledges that God is always with him and will never leave him and because of that he worships Him.

Matt 28:20," And remember, I am with you always, to the end of the age."

"Oh Timeless-One,
I know you are with me.
I know you are beside me.
I know you dwell in me.

Oh, Timeless-One,
I heart-link with you.
I worship only you,
I will die for you."

This is a song by Caleb of adoration and praise to the Timeless-One after defeating Baphomet.

Ps 121:2," My help comes from the LORD, the Creator of heaven and earth!"

Isa 40:28, "Do you not know? Have you not heard? The LORD is an eternal God, the creator of the whole earth. He does not get tired or weary; there is no limit to his wisdom."

"Before darkness covered the endless space,
Before your angels sang songs of praise,
You are.

Before you created air,
Before you called for sound,
Before you hung one star,
Before you made one heart to pound,
You are.
Glory to the Timeless-One."

After heart-linking with the Timeless-One, the Lord breathed on Caleb and empowered him by the Holy Spirit. Caleb then sang this song of praise.

Gen 2:7 So the Lord God formed the man from the dust of the ground, breathed life into his lungs, and the man became a living being.

> "Oh, how great is Your love for your servant,
> You breathed on me and gave me power.
> You touched my mind and gave me peace,
> You broke my heart and made me whole.
> Life, love and joy, You have given me,
> With the Fire of Your Spirit
> You restored my soul,
> Holy, Holy, Holy
> To the Timeless-One."

After defeating Mr. Wizard, Caleb sang a song of thanksgiving and praise.

Ps 23:4 Yea, though I walk through the valley of the shadow of death, I will fear no evil; for You are with me; Your rod and Your staff, they comfort me.

> "You never forget your servant,
> You never forsake your child,
> You're with me in the calm times,
> You're with me in the trial.
>
> Blessed is the Timeless-One,
> Blessed is your name,
> Blessed is the Timeless-One,
> Holy is Your name.
>
> You delivered me from evil,
> You delivered me from pain,

You sheltered me from death,
You are the only way."

Songs
And
Prayers
From
The Black Dome

After hearing of his brother being trapped in the Black Dome, Caleb heart-linked, then sings a song to the Timeless-One.

Ps 121:2 My help comes from the LORD, the Creator of heaven and earth!

Rev 1:8 "I am the Alpha and the Omega," says the Lord God – the one who is, and who was, and who is still to come – the All-Powerful!

"Oh Timeless-One,
Creator of all,
Full of power,
I hear the call.

You have no beginning,
You have no end,
You are wisdom,
On you I depend."

Camping at a safe distance from the Black Dome, Caleb reads from the Holy Verses. Then Caleb and the men join in a sacred song for deliverance.

Ps 28:9 Deliver your people! Empower the nation that belongs to you! Care for them like a shepherd and carry them in your arms at all times!

> "Oh Timeless-One,
> Oh, Holy One,
> Carry us through,
> And guide our swords.
>
> Oh, Timeless-One,
> Power and Spirit,
> Lift us up,
> Bring the enemy to their knees."

Caleb and the men sing a song of thanksgiving after the rescue of Logan and others.

Ps 17:7 Accomplish awesome, faithful deeds, you who powerfully deliver those who look to you for protection from their enemies.

Rev 15:3 They sang the song of Moses the servant of God and the song of the Lamb: "Great and astounding are your deeds, Lord God, the All-Powerful! Just and true are your ways, King over the nations!

> "Great and powerful are you Timeless-One.
> You deliver us,
> And never tire.
> Holy and Worthy of praise,
> We shout for joy,
> You hear us,
> We give you the Glory."

Songs
and
Prayers
from
The Fire

Caleb leads a village in a song of thanksgiving and praise.

Luke 3:16 John answered them all, "I baptize you with water, but one more powerful than I am is coming – I am not worthy to untie the strap of his sandals. He will baptize you with the Holy Spirit and fire.

"Oh, Timeless-One.
We felt the fire of your love,
We can smell the incense
Of your glory.

We thank you for our deliverance.
We thank you for your love.
We give you thanks Mighty One,
We give you thanks and lift You up."

Songs
and
Prayers
from
The Contest

Caleb led his holy regime in a song soon after leaving for battle.

John 3:8 The wind blows wherever it will, and you hear the sound it makes, but do not know where it comes from and where it is going. So it is with everyone who is born of the Spirit."

Ps 16:11 You lead me in the path of life; I experience absolute joy in your presence; you always give me sheer delight.

"You cause the wind to blow,
And we follow.
You cause the sun to shine,
And we run.
Ten thousand miles is just
A step away.
Tomorrow we see is just
A breath away.

Oh, we follow
You lead.
Oh, we listen
You speak.
Oh, we cling
You hold.
We love
You more and more."

Wah'li'si desiring a deeper relationship with God, she speaks to Him passionately ready for the visit of the Holy Spirit.

Ezek 37:9 He said to me, "Prophesy to the breath, – prophesy, son of man – and say to the breath: 'This is what the sovereign LORD says: Come from the four winds, O breath, and breathe on these corpses so that they may live.'"

John 20:21 So Jesus said to them again, "Peace be with you. Just as the Father has sent me, I also send you."

John 20:22 And after he said this, he breathed on them and said, "Receive the Holy Spirit.

> "Breathe unto me love,
> Breathe unto me life.
> Breathe unto me desire.
> Breathe unto me fire.
> Breathe unto me life."

Then the Lord answered her saying:

> "Woman, I see in you
> a passion to sing,
> a passion to dance,
> a passion to praise
> a passion, a radiance.
> I will bless you and give you your heart's desire."

Wah'li'si blessed and full of the Spirit spoke to the Lord again.

> "Blessed art thou O Lord,
> Blessed and holy.
> Blessed is He who sits on the throne,
> With power and glory.
> Oh, a holy wonderment."

Now, Wah'li'si breaks out in song and dance.

> "Holy Wonderment,
> A mystery, oh majesty.
> Holy Wonderment,
> A might King. The Prince of Peace.
> Holy Wonderment,
> The Rock did bleed. A Savior indeed.
> Holy Wonderment."

Caleb and Wah'li'si lead the others in a song of praise as the Timeless-One shelters them from evil.

Ps 91:2 I say this about the LORD, my shelter and my stronghold, my God in whom I trust –

Ps 91:3 he will certainly rescue you from the snare of the hunter and from the destructive plague.

Ps 91:4 He will shelter you with his wings; you will find safety under his wings. His faithfulness is like a shield or a protective wall.

> "You shelter your servants
> With your mighty wings.
> You hide us in the
> Cleft of the Rock.
> We walk in the midst
> Of your glory.
> Your Spirit has given us
> A champions heart."

At the contest Wah'li'si began dancing in the Spirit, then broke out in praise and worship.

Ps 63:4 For this reason I will praise you while I live; in your name I will lift up my hands.

1Tim 2:8 So I want the men to pray in every place, lifting up holy hands without anger or dispute.

"Lift up your voice,
Lift up your heads,
Lift up your hearts,
Oh, let's dance.

"Feel, feel the Spirit,
Oh, feel the Fire,
Feel, feel the music,
Oh, take the power.

"Come, come Holy Spirit,
Come into this house.
Come, come Holy Spirit,
Come into Your house."

Songs
and
Prayers
from
The Sound of Silence

After traveling back in time and space and after spending time in Heaven talking to Jesus, Caleb prayed this prayer.

Rev 1:8 "I am the Alpha and the Omega," says the Lord God – the one who is, and who was, and who is still to come – the All-Powerful!

Rev 21:6 He also said to me, "It is done! I am the Alpha and the Omega, the beginning and the end. To the one who is thirsty I will give water free of charge from the spring of the water of life.

"Oh, Timeless-One,
All power and glory belongs to you.
Oh, Timeless-One,
You are before time. You will be after time.
At your Word, time obeys.
Oh, guide your servant.
Lead me down the right path.
Fill your servant with every right word,
Oh, Timeless-One,
All power and all glory belong to you!"

For encouragement, Caleb prayed this prayer.

Isa 6:1 In the year of King Uzziah's death, I saw the sovereign master seated on a high, elevated throne. The hem of his robe filled the temple.

Isa 6:2 Seraphs stood over him; each one had six wings. With two wings they covered their faces, with two they covered their feet, and they used the remaining two to fly.

Isa 6:3 They called out to one another, "Holy, holy, holy is the Lord who commands armies! His majestic splendor fills the entire earth!"

Isa 6:4 The sound of their voices shook the door frames, and the temple was filled with smoke.

Isa 6:5, I said, "Too bad for me! I am destroyed, for my lips are contaminated by sin, and I live among people whose lips are contaminated by sin. My eyes have seen the king, the LORD who commands armies."

Isa 6:6 But then one of the seraphs flew toward me. In his hand was a hot coal he had taken from the altar with tongs.

Isa 6:7 He touched my mouth with it and said, "Look, this coal has touched your lips. Your evil is removed; your sin is forgiven."

Isa 6:8 I heard the voice of the sovereign master say, "Whom will I send? Who will go on our behalf?" I answered, "Here I am, send me!"

"Oh Timeless-One
I am here. You are here.
You called, I came.

"You touched my soul,
With the Holy Ember,
And filled my eyes with Fire.

"I know, You know
My heart, Your temple.

Selah……Amen!"

Caleb prays for rest and protection.

Matt 11:28 Come to me, all you who are weary and burdened, and I will give you rest.

Matt 11:29 Take my yoke on you and learn from me, because I am gentle and humble in heart, and you will find rest for your souls.

Matt 11:30 For my yoke is easy to bear, and my load is not hard to carry."

"Hear O Lord of all,
Hear your servant call from the past.
I call from a time that has already been
To the God that always shall be.
Give me rest.
Cover me with Your mighty wings."

Caleb prays for those in darkness.

John 8:12 Then Jesus spoke out again, "I am the light of the world. The one who follows me will never walk in darkness, but will have the light of life."

<blockquote>
"Oh, Timeless-One
Show your great and awesome power
To those who are in darkness
Show Your light."
</blockquote>

Songs

and

Prayers

from

Rhyme Riddles and Reason

Rejoicing after defeating the man of deception with a war of words, Caleb sang this song.

Rev 4:8 Each one of the four living creatures had six wings and was full of eyes all around and inside. They never rest day or night, saying: "Holy Holy Holy is the Lord God, the All-Powerful, Who was and who is, and who is still to come!"

<blockquote>
"Most High, You are
Most ancient and holy.
Most blessed You are,
Most loving and righteous."
</blockquote>

Songs
and
Prayers
from
The Garden

Caleb offers up a song of praise to the Timeless-One.

John 12:13 So they took branches of palm trees and went out to meet him. They began to shout, "Hosanna! Blessed is the one who comes in the name of the Lord! Blessed is the king of Israel!"

1Pet 1:3 Blessed be the God and Father of our Lord Jesus Christ! By his great mercy he gave us new birth into a living hope through the resurrection of Jesus Christ from the dead,

> "Your glory is here.
> Your power is great.
> Your Spirit shines,
> And You are never late.
> "Blessed be the name of the Lord,
> Blessed is the Lord Most High,
> Blessed is the Ancient of Days,
> Blessed are You, Oh, God!"

Wah'li'si prays a prayer of protection over Jessica and Petra.

Ps 139:5-10 "You squeeze me in from behind and in front; you place your hand on me. Your knowledge is beyond my comprehension; it is so far beyond me, I am unable to fathom it. Where can I go to escape your spirit? Where can I flee to escape your presence? If I were to ascend to heaven, you would be there. If I were to sprawl out in Sheol, there you would be. If I were to fly away on the wings of the dawn, and settle down on the other side of the sea, even there your hand would guide me, your right hand would grab hold of me."

> "Mighty God,
> Ruler of the universe and beyond.
> Strong in battle, power with no end
> With the hands that hold the lightening
> …Hold the weak
> With the arms that threw the stars in space,
> …Hold the weak
> With the breast that hold the breath of life,
> …Hold the weak.
> Selah, Amen."

Before leaving on their journey, Caleb said a short prayer.

John 1:15 John testified about him and shouted out, "This one was the one about whom I said, 'He who comes after me is greater than I am, because he existed before me.'"

Ps 16:9-11 So my heart rejoices and I am happy; My life is safe. You will not abandon me to Sheol; you will not allow your faithful follower to see the Pit. You lead me in the path of life; I experience absolute joy in your presence; you always give me sheer delight.

> "Oh, Timeless-One,
> Where we go, You have already been,
> You go before us and clear a path,
> We walk in Your way,

Victory is the only end."

An angelic choir sings.

Rev 4:8 Each one of the four living creatures had six wings and was full of eyes all around and inside. They never rest day or night, saying: "Holy Holy Holy is the Lord God, the All-Powerful, Who was and who is, and who is still to come!"

"Holy, holy, holy,
The Lord is full of glory.
Oh, Holy Warrior,
You alone are holy."

The Timeless-One speaks to them.

Ps 1:1-2 How blessed is the one who does not follow the advice of the wicked, or stand in the pathway with sinners, or sit in the assembly of scoffers!Instead he finds pleasure in obeying the LORD's commands; he meditates on his commands day and night.

"Blessed are You,
And anointed.
Blessed are You
And sealed.
Blessed are You,
And filled."

The Timeless-One continues speaking.
"Go to battle,
And win.
Go to rescue,
And save,

Go to conquer
And destroy."

After being blessed by the Lord, Wah'li'si and Ovation sing this song.

Ps 150:6 Let everything that has breath praise the LORD! Praise the LORD!

"The Word is our song,
Salvation is our strength
Your Spirit moves in us,
Like a dancing flame.

The heavens open up
To show your wonders.
You made the universe,
Hold me in your arms like a new born.
Praise the Lord,
All that breathe,
Praise the Lord,
And never cease."
(repeat)

The Lord gave them victory so Caleb prayed a prayer of thanksgiving.

Ps 24:7 Look up, you gates! Rise up, you eternal doors! Then the majestic king will enter!

"We give thanks to you,
Oh, Timeless-One.
You have shown us mercy,
And much love.
We give you praise,
And worship only You.
You are the victor,
Once again, King of Glory.
Amen."

Wah'li'si tells Diana and Lilith and Rhiannon about the Lord in song.

Ps 115:15 May you be blessed by the LORD, the creator of heaven and earth!

"He is the creator of the universe.
He is the lover of my soul.
He fills me with His Spirit.
He cleans me with His blood.

"He calls to the lonely.
He calls to the lost.
He says, 'I love you.
I love you at all cost.'"

After Diana, Lilith and Rhiannon became followers of the Timeless-One, Ovation led in a song of rejoicing.

Jas 1:12 Happy is the one who endures testing, because when he has proven to be genuine, he will receive the crown of life that God promised to those who love him.

"Add another seat to the table,
Another mansion is being built,
Another crown is being made,
Add one more name to the book.

"Glory, glory, glory
Glory to the Lamb.
Holy, holy, holy,
Holy is the Lamb.
(chorus)
"Welcome to the family of God,

Your sins are washed away,
Welcome to the family of God,
Your lives will never be the same."
(chorus)

Songs
and
Prayers
from
Liquid Christ

A prayer by Caleb of worship and praise.

Ps 23:5 You prepare a feast before me in plain sight of my enemies. You refresh my head with oil; my cup is completely full.

Heb 1:9 You have loved righteousness and hated lawlessness. So God, your God, has anointed you over your companions with the oil of rejoicing."

"Oh, Timeless-One
With your sweet anointing oil
You bathe me.
With your sweet Holy Spirit
You baptize me.

"Wisdom is so precious,
She is so lovely.
She is so gentle.
And so full of power.

"Oh, Lord full of glory,
You have illuminated my soul

And enlightened my mind.
You have filled my heart with love,
And my eyes with fire.

Blessed be the name of the Lord,
Blessed is the Lord Most High
Blessed is the Ancient of Days.
Blessed are You oh, God."

Caleb sings and sings songs of praise and worship.

"Lord of heaven and earth,
God of the universe and beyond,
Ruler of the galaxies,
Lord of host You are."
(repeat)

A praise and worship by Wah'li'si.

Isa 6:3 They called out to one another, "Holy, holy, holy is the Lord who commands armies! His majestic splendor fills the entire earth!"

"Holy is the Lord
And worthy to be praised
Holy is the Lord
His majesty reigns.

"He's shown us a mystery,
He's shown us truth
He's given us wisdom
And made our hearts brand new.

"Oh the mystery of your love,

The hidden treasures of your heart.
One ounce of Your living water,
Satisfies a thousand galaxies.

Selah, amen.
Everyone, amen."

Songs
and
Prayers
from
Corridors

A statement from Caleb.

Prov 24:5 A wise warrior is strong, and a man of knowledge makes his strength stronger;

"To be tested,
Is to be made strong.
To be attacked,
Is to crush the head of Satan."

Caleb and his holy regime sing a song of worship.

"Holy, holy, holy,
The Lord is full of glory.
Holy, holy, holy,
Our Promise,
Our Star of the Morning."

Caleb speaks to Heaven.

Ps 17:8 Protect me as you would protect the pupil of your eye! Hide me in the shadow of your wings!

> "When morning breaks,
> You greet us with heaven's kiss.
> At the heat of noonday,
> The shade of heaven's wings.
> When night falls,
> Your songs of love and grace
> Comfort us."

Caleb says a prayer of praise and thanksgiving.

Ps 3:7-8 Rise up, LORD! Deliver me, my God! Yes, you will strike all my enemies on the jaw; you will break the teeth of the wicked. The LORD delivers; you show favor to your people. (Selah)

> "Oh Timeless-One.,
> Again you delivered us.
> Again you came to our rescue.
>
> "You carried us.
> You sheltered our souls.
> And cleansed us in your blood.
>
> Full of power, honor and glory.
>
> Amen.
> Everyone, amen."

Songs
and
Prayers
from
The Psalmus

The Psalmus, a wise elderly man, giving words of encouragement and wisdom to Caleb.

1Cor 10:31 So whether you eat or drink, or whatever you do, do everything for the glory of God.

"Let every breath you take,
Every word you speak,
Every line you pen,
Let every heartbeat
Every wink of the eye,
Every word uttered,
Let every action and reaction
Be for the Lord Most High."

The Psalmus encourages Caleb again.

Rom 16:20 The God of peace will quickly crush Satan under your feet. The grace of our Lord Jesus be with you.

"When the littlest of gods
Raises his sword of hate
Against you
And spews his blackened fire
From his eyes
To blind you.

"Shout the Word!
Cry out the Name!
Lift you heel,
And crush his head!

The Lord your God is
With you."

Caleb responded to the Psalmus with much joy and gladness.

"Blessed is the Lord Most High,
Words from the Word.
Through a willing vessel.
Amen."

Caleb speaks to the Psalmus.

Matt 5:6 "Blessed are those who hunger and thirst for righteousness, for they will be satisfied.

"Secret ears long to hear,
Hidden hearts long to be filled.
Anxious eyes yearn to see,
And lonely lips hunger to praise."

The Psalmus replies.

Isa 61:3 to provide for those who grieve in Zion— to bestow on them a crown of beauty instead of ashes, the oil of gladness instead of mourning, a mantle of praise instead of a spirit of despair." "Then people will call them "Oaks of Righteousness", "The Planting of the Lord", in order to display his splendor.

"As mourning is turned to praise,
And night is turned to day.
The hungry shall be filled,
And the dying shall be saved."

"Let it be so. Amen,"

said, Caleb.

The Word speaks to Caleb and The Psalmus about the mightiness of the Holy Spirit.

> "The Son shines on the wicked and the righteous.
> Yet the wicked does not see it.
> The Spirit moves across the land
> Like a mighty whirlwind.
> The righteous stand in the midst of it and say, 'Fill us, fill us.'
> The wicked runs and hides in caves."

Then the Word spoke again of the power of the Holy Spirit.

> "As the Fire moves like a hurricane,
> And purifies all it touches.
> The wicked crawls under rocks for cover.
> The righteous say, 'Consume us.'"

The Word looked at Caleb with His eyes full of love and penetrating fire and said, "Caleb."

Caleb didn't look up but said, "Yes Lord?"

"Until the days are complete," said the Word. "Where will you be?"

Caleb answered, "Here serving You."

Again, the Word said, "As the day draws nearer, where will you be?"

Caleb answered, "Here on this earth serving only You."

The Word questioned again, "Tell me, when the day of completeness arrives, then what?"

Keeping his head down and not looking up, Caleb answered saying, "To be transformed and leave this place. To be where You are."

The Word smiled and when He smiled, his eyes smiled with Him and He said, "Oh, Caleb, I love you. When that day comes, you will. You shall be with me, forever."

Until our Lord returns for us, let us serve Him with fervent love and great compassion spreading the Good News.

> "Before the foundation of
> the galaxies were laid,
> The Timeless-One looked
> across time and saw you.
> And He smiled."

WHAT IS OUTCAST NATION?

The OutCast Nation is a place for believers to be inspired, encouraged and to learn who they are in Christ and Who God is. It is to be a light in the darkness for those who don't yet believe.

OutCast Nation came from the scripture Micah 4:7 where it says in the New American Standard version.

Mic 4:7 "I will make the lame a remnant and the outcasts a strong nation,"

Mic 4:7 "I will make the lame, the defective a remnant and a survivor. I will make the outcasts, the freaks, the misfits, the rejects and discarded ones a strong nation and a massive powerful variety of people,"

(OutCast Version)

This scripture is relevant for what I am using it for.

God's restoration isn't just for the strong, but the weak and disadvantaged will especially know the blessing of His restoration.

Who are the Outcasts today? They are the discarded ones, The Misfits, The Freaks, The Goths, the ones who keep messing up repeatedly, like me. They are the ones who dress differently, talk differently, listen to different kinds of music. Maybe we wear too much black, maybe we like skulls too much. Tattooed, Body piercings.

They may have blue, green, purple, pink hair or no hair. But do you know what? Man looks on the outward appearance, but God looks at the heart.

Whatever we look like on the outside is not important. What is important is Who is on the inside. That is what Father God is looking at. He is looking to see Jesus in you, not our clothes and make-up and hair color.

1Sa 16:7 But the LORD said to Samuel, "Do not look at his appearance or at the height of his stature, because I have rejected him; for God sees not as man sees, for man looks at the outward appearance, but the LORD looks at the heart."

OutCast Nation is here to share who you are in Jesus Christ, and who you can be. And who you are not.

Outwardly, yes, we are all freaks, but who are we in Jesus?

Our identity is in Jesus.

OutCast Nation is about learning what and who we are as Brand-New Creations.

OutCast Nation is about leaving our past in the past and learning that the Bible says that our past was erased and changed. That we are to move forward.

God is making this OutCast Nation into a strong nation.

Following my wife and I's time as House Parents for at-risk teen girls, the Lord led me to start OutCast Nation. The girls were in the system for multiple reasons. They lived very violent lives. Some use to live in cars. Some were sold for drugs, raped by family members and many other horrible things. The Lord gave me a message for them, and that was - their identity is in Christ, and how Jesus thinks of them. Their past doesn't define who they are. Let the past die and let Jesus heal them. It really made a difference in them.

When our time was up, I didn't know what to do. I, myself didn't feel like I was finished. I felt the Lord leading me to go this route to share the message that He gave me for the girls. To share this message with the Gothic community, to the Freaks, to the Weird and Strange ones, to the discarded ones and the rejects, to the OutCasts of the Church and society. At least that's where it started. Though, it has evolved into something larger, something greater.

The OutCast Nation began as an outreach for those who don't feel welcomed at the traditional Church. And, for those who keep messing-up repeatedly like me. God is the God of second, third, fourth...chances. I myself don't really feel welcomed in some Churches.

The Outcast Nation is a diverse nation, and a strong nation.

When the Outcast Nation started, I never would have dreamed there would be such a diverse number of people following the page. Teachers, Preachers, Musicians, Evangelist, Psychiatrists, Witches, Goths, Punks, Straight, Gay and so on.

We may be OutCasts to the Church and the world, but we are God's OutCasts that He has made into a Strong Nation.

Luke 14:23, 24 "So the master told him, 'All right. Go out again, and this time bring them all back with you. Persuade the beggars on the streets, the hookers on the street corners and their pimps, the outcasts, the freaks and the rejects, who live in the shadows, even the homeless. Urgently insist that they come in My house and enjoy the feast so that my house will be full of joy.'

"I say to you all, the one who receives the invitation to My feast with me and makes excuse after excuse will never enjoy my banquet."

(OutCast Version)

All are invited.

God has done a great and mighty work here. I give Father God Who is the Timeless-One all the Glory. I am nothing without Him. I can do nothing without Him.

Soon, I pray God will give me the means to open an actual Church building.

The root message Father God gave me for the OutCast Nation is, 1. who we are in Christ, 2. leave the past behind, 3. we are new, never existed before creations, 4. Father God loves us, He calls us His Segullah (Hebrew meaning, His Special Possession and Treasured Jewel), 5. Father God is Jealous for us because His Name is Jealous- Exo 34:14, 6. Father God has engraved us in the palms of His hands, He never leaves us Isa 49:16, 7. Father God is NOT a scary, mean or an angry God. He is a loving, tender and caring Father, 8. Father God cares about the condition of the heart, not our appearance (not what we wear or look like).

As I said, I believe this is a message that needs to be heard. It's been two years since I started the OutCast Nation page on Facebook, and the page now has over 1200 followers. So, I am trying to get the financial means to get an actual Church building under the same name, so all of us OutCasts will have a place to go where we can be who God made us to be.

https://www.facebook.com/ChurchoftheOutcast

ABOUT THE AUTHOR

Daniel Riffe lives in Monett Missouri. He has two daughters and five grandchildren. He is a musician and song writer. He has studied the occult, Satanism and witchcraft from a Christian point of view and has given talks to youth groups on the dangers of secular rock music and the occult. He is the founder and pastor of OutCast Nation ministries. OutCast Nation is a ministry for the goths, the freaks, the rejected and discarded ones for being different, and for those who don't feel welcomed in the traditional church.

His passion is the OutCast Nation, writing praise and worship and **knowing** God and the Bible like never before. He can be reached at, **PastorDWRiffe@outlook.com**.

Printed by Libri Plureos GmbH in Hamburg, Germany